About the Author

JW Garfield began university playing (American) football and running track until a severe injury halted his pursuit of athletics. Since the injury, JW Garfield has dedicated himself to academics. He is currently a PhD candidate studying vertebral fracture mechanics and has five articles published in scientific journals. In addition, JW Garfield writes for his university's newspaper and monthly literary magazine, and he likes to spend his free time reading about new and exciting historical contexts for novels. Crooked Taylor is JW Garfield's first published novel.

Crooked Taylor

JW Garfield

Crooked Taylor

Olympia Publishers
London

www.olympiapublishers.com
OLYMPIA PAPERBACK EDITION

Copyright © JW Garfield 2023

The right of JW Garfield to be identified as author of
this work has been asserted in accordance with sections 77 and 78 of
the Copyright, Designs and Patents Act 1988.

All Rights Reserved

No reproduction, copy or transmission of this publication
may be made without written permission.
No paragraph of this publication may be reproduced,
copied or transmitted save with the written permission of the publisher,
or in accordance with the provisions
of the Copyright Act 1956 (as amended).

Any person who commits any unauthorised act in relation to
this publication may be liable to criminal
prosecution and civil claims for damage.

A CIP catalogue record for this title is
available from the British Library.

ISBN: 978-1-80074-675-6

This is a work of fiction.
Names, characters, places and incidents originate from the writer's
imagination. Any resemblance to actual persons, living or dead, is
purely coincidental.

First Published in 2023

Olympia Publishers
Tallis House
2 Tallis Street
London
EC4Y 0AB

Printed in Great Britain

Dedication

Crooked Taylor is dedicated to my parents. Your support is inexhaustible, and your love knows no bounds. John Graham, and Wendy Patricia, this book is for you.

Acknowledgements

I want to acknowledge the Olympia publishing team for their efforts in bringing Crooked Taylor to print.
First, I want to thank Ms. Alison Payne for her valuable edits to the manuscript.
Second, I want to thank Ms. Kristina Smith for all her assistance throughout the publishing process.
Last, I want to thank Mr. James Houghton for the opportunity to publish *Crooked* Taylor with Olympia Publishers.
Thank you to everyone involved in the process of bringing *Crooked* Taylor to life; I am confident that he will not let you down.

"Sometimes to see things straight, you gotta be a little *crooked*."
— Bradley Taylor —

One

The sun announced itself long before its arrival in the sky, beginning with a slow retreat in the density of the night. Black velvet clouds loosened and broke apart like smoke in a wind, giving way to a gunmetal morning that, once gray, accelerated toward dawn with a rapid reddening of the world, before the sun's first golden spears struck the sky like broad strokes of lightning.

Traffic in the streets accumulated in proportion to the brightness of the day, and full dawn saw dirt avenues choked with citizens all flowing in a single direction. Horses snuffled and wagon wheels wobbled and clattered, and a haze of grit as fine as chalk dust was raised from the mass disturbance of the city. People clustered on the steps of the church, and like the satellite camps of travelers that dotted the plains outside of town, small groups began to form in which pipes and cigarettes were produced.

The groups grew in size and number, and the people occupying these groups were too eclectic for description, other than to testify that every corner of the great frontier had seemingly sent forth an ambassador. Buffalo hunters could be observed stripping skins as the day warmed them beneath their piles of hides. A tinker conducted nonchalant business by permitting his overcoat to hang loose about him, so that whenever he turned it would flap open to expose some of the wares overflowing his myriad pockets.

A man equipped with an equal number of teeth and eyes bawled laughter and raised a flask above his head, and someone nearby cussed at him and told him to cap it.

"Blow it!" the man called. The person who had directed his flask's capping was no longer paying attention, so the comment was lost among the many other conversations taking place. The church bell tolled its first of the day, but the crowd ignored its calling.

"—spring right off them. That awkward plant and leap, never seen anything like it in my life—"

"Joel!" The man with two teeth turned from his guests and, recognizing a friend, admitted him into their circle by stepping aside.

"Morning, Peter."

"Morning."

Peter stepped shoulder-up to Joel, then focused his attention on the other three men. Two he recognized. He shook Moses Louis-May's hand, followed by Ed Broadstreet's, and quickly inquired regarding the wives and children of each, before turning his attention to the third — whose mustache was the most lopsided Peter had ever seen. He tried not to stare while he was introduced, but it seemed to be combed over from one side of his lip toward the other in the most curious fashion.

"Peter Eckhart, this is Lieutenant Sinaloa. We were just talking, he fought Crooked up in the territories in forty-two and I was telling him how he used his crutches because Mark here—"

"Mark?"

"Mark Sinaloa. Mother's American."

"Uh," Peter nodded, then Joel said,

"So, Lieutenant here, he saw him, or we think so. Sounds like it, but he never saw him on foot, only on horseback. You could never tell if it was Crooked from horseback. Nothing special. Normal face, not especially big or tall or special-looking, hard to tell except up close. On the ground though, he was born with legs that looked like you took a warm candle and bent it all out of shape. They could support him, hold him up, but they looked like these skinny twisted white candles about to give way any second. They seemed durable enough. I was telling Mark, the way you could tell it was Crooked Taylor was that when he was on crutches, he'd do this sort of forward leap where he'd throw himself at his crutches and plant them, then swing his little lower body through like the pendulum of some crazy grandfather clock and launch himself and land and spring off those twisted little legs and vault onto his crutches again. He could travel as fast as a regular man could at a jog, or almost I'd say."

"Where'd you encounter him?" Peter asked Mark Sinaloa's mustache before relocating his eyes to the speaker's and trying to do a better job of listening.

"We departed from Fort Orre in Missouri, though I reckon we were damn near to Mexico by the time we actually found him. I was second-in-command of a band of prisoners we had picked over a coupla weeks, ranging up through the Silver Mountains, which I like to call the Silver Hills because I don't think the people naming them quite knew real mountains..."

Two

The troop was already in a bad way when they pushed into the mountains, but the intention was to skirt a couple hundred miles of wide-open terrain across which the laws of man were unknown. A landscape composed only of desert, hardship, and uncertainty.

But ascending the mountain became more treacherous by the hour, and the first night brought a storm where lightning forked inches above the tips of the pines, and thunder sounded too frequently to be counted. The going was slow, and Captain Montre ordered the prisoners be unchained so that they might accelerate their pace. The storm was so vicious that rather than ponder escape, the unchained men looked inward and fled that turbulent night into the sanctuary of their soul and whatever safe harbor their god could grant them in that terrible hour.

One of the guards, nicknamed Cigarillo for his small cock, pulled out his pistol and fired into the night, his terror so great he felt as though by producing some audible calamity — something over which he had power and control — he might remain sane during the storm.

The horses had been hobbled, but they still reared and snapped their jaws and kicked their hooves as best they could. One of them had its rear hip broken during the fracas and lay on its side as the hooves and the mud and the rain fell in a violent deluge upon it, and the thunder was so great that the violence of the struggle was inaudible.

With God's eye squarely scowled at them the men hunkered down in their cold camp as best they could, but the morning saw no release from the bad weather, and so they mounted up and continued in sheeting rain.

Cigarillo and Parks rode double, because that morning it was Cigarillo's horse they found moaning like a corpse and blowing bubbles in the mud with its snout. Cigarillo had to put it down with his knife because his pistol was soaked through and in the icy downpour no piece could be disassembled and oiled.

The horse's blood exited its throat in a ribbon of gore, and Cigarillo caught much of it in his canteen and drank some and passed around the rest. Mark remembered his hunger, he remembered the iron in the horse blood as he drank it, and he remembered Alcion Carter kneeling in the puddle of gore and sucking at the wound in the animal's neck like a perverse and starving vampire.

The rain was a constant sheet of water, and the convicts also drank blood from the horse and choice cuts were extracted, but there was no time for a full cleaning, so much of the bounty was left to the wolves.

The second day in the mountains the rain only subsided when a cold north wind ushered it past. The temperature plummeted and at no point since the thunderstorm did Captain Montre ever link the six convicts together again, for each prisoner knew in their heart that their greatest chance for survival lay in remaining with their captors.

The cold wind brought fat flakes that spun and circled in the gray air, and clouds billowed like a house fire as their charcoal mass accumulated across the horizon. Captain Montre ordered the wagon to be abandoned, and he strapped supplies to each of the convicts and used them similarly to the mule that was cut free and piled with baggage until its belly nearly dragged.

The storm worsened all afternoon. The wind moaned and whistled in the jagged teeth of the passes like some megalithic beast, and pine trees shivered free of their downy coats of snow. Mark squinted past the line of convicts toward the strung-out positions of their bedraggled troupe, the end of which he could not even see through the sheets of snow billowing in the wind like mainsails.

Lieutenant Sinaloa had his horse's reins looped around the wrists of his leather gloves; his arms buried in the folds of his entire wardrobe. Soaked through, he was wearing every article of clothing he owned in an attempt to keep the cold from claiming him. His horse Catalan could not lift her hooves free of the snowdrifts, and the wagon path was long since lost, necessitating Catalan to bull her way sternum-first through the powder and blaze a trail for the rest.

The first shot could have been mistaken for a frozen tree bursting from cold sap expanding in its veins. But there was little time for the first shot to be registered before the next arrived, and at this most inopportune time a gust of snow caught Mark in the face, blinding him, as someone behind him cried out in pain.

Mark's horse reared then jerked unnaturally, and as she spun Catalan sprouted blood from her blond side, and Mark began to detach from his saddle, but not before she fell on him and let loose another scream. Catalan fell on her side and Mark thanked Madre Maria for a soft landing in the snow that allowed him to crawl free uninjured. Catalan kicked and squirmed and rose to her feet, but Mark stayed on his knees and pulled his colt from its holster, cursing his rifle for being in his saddle scabbard.

Glass was still upon his horse, whirling about, the reins trailing as he aimed his rifle into the blinding storm and spooked at every ghost that swirled among the trees. His horse was shot and he with it, and Glass tumbled sideways from his horse as the frightened creature took flight. The bleeding horse crashed into the trees ahead and was lost and Mark followed the gasping powder in its wake but saw nothing. To his left rifle fire blinked and Mark ducked. He fell and snow burst in his face and the rifle shot was lost amidst the chaos and Mark knew not its impact. He got to his knees and pulled the colt, and the howling of crazed men closed in and reverberated among the slashing waves of snow and wind.

Bandits all in white appeared from the trees and their guns crackled without pause as the attackers fired at will. Glass was on his feet, and his pelts burst red all about him as he returned fire and hit nothing. He did not stand against the volley long and was soon sent tumbling into a red drift of snow.

Mark fired and hit a man in the knee and then was pierced in his side before his head jerked about and he fell face down in the snow again. Mark winced and when he breathed, he felt as though a hot poker was stuck in his side. He tried to rise but the pain flared, and his vision spotted from the effort. Below his face the snow was warm, and blood was flowing at an alarming rate. He felt his mouth, and the gunfire ceased, and the weight of the twilight's silence fell upon him like an avalanche.

"On your knees! Wrangle them up, I'm not trudging over there to give each and every one a handshake!"

Mark raised his head and Captain Montre was on his knees, groaning, and only able to hold one hand above his head, while two of the bandits stood near him, one of them smoking. The rest of the attackers quickly materialized from the trees and entered the clearing to search the bodies.

Mark began to crawl, but he was well within the

circumference of the fight, so he laid down his head and tried to ignore the bleeding from his mouth. A brief survey with his fingertips left him alarmed at how little upper lip he had left, but the sound of footsteps was loud enough, crunching in the swirling drifts of snow, that he put down his head and watched the snow melt beneath his face as he prayed that he would not be found.

The weather had taken its toll on these men too, despite their superior preparation, and nearby, Mark believed it was Cigarillo's voice who screamed, "No, don't! I surren—!" but was cut short by a knife, jammed to the hilt in his throat and twisted, so that when it was retrieved there was a cavern of gore through which Cigarillo could do nothing but gurgle. The bandits began to strip Cigarillo before he was even dead, tugging at his jacket and furs while he fumbled uselessly at the wound in his neck with his fingers.

Mark figured it was a combination of the extent to which they were wounded and the desirability of their kit, but some men were executed immediately, while a couple of others were brought together, huddled on their knees side-by-side below the horse of Crooked Taylor.

When a bandit approached him, Mark went limp, and the sound of more executions in the clearing encouraged Mark to ignore the profuse bleeding from his facial wound. It was this bleeding however, combined with the blood that seeped through his jacket from being shot in the back, that convinced the bandit that Mark did not need to be killed any more than he already was, and also had nothing valuable in his possession. The bandit passed him by, and the snow gusted, and Mark heard its icy droplets needling against the stiff, frozen denim of the man's bleach-white pants.

The bleeding had not lessened, but the bandits and Crooked

Taylor stood much too near for Mark to feel safe in turning his head. Instead, he watched the red trough beneath his face that his blood was digging with its warmth, while his toes and fingers stiffened as though the meat on his bones was slowly freezing solid.

Mark lay in the agony of his wounds and listened to the executions occur thirty feet away. Perhaps even twenty-five.

"State your name and how much you're worth," Crooked instructed. Most of the prisoners being transported by Mark had survived, but they were reluctant to speak about their crimes and incentivize a bounty that would see them brought to the nearest town and hanged. Crooked clarified by adding, "We just got done killing half a dozen rangers. I'm not welcome to ride into town and claim a bounty, I wanna know if anyone here is worth keeping with us and feeding, or if you ain't even worth the price of a bullet and we need to just leave you here as-is."

"I'm worth a hundred dollars!" A man offered. A true amount, for Mark knew the bounty allocated for each of the six criminals, four of whom had survived the fight.

Crooked replied to the hundred-dollar claim, by pulling the trigger of his Winchester Repeater and centering a bullet in the man's chest. Mark believed that William Garvey was the first man shot. It seemed that Crooked had not liked what he saw.

"I'm worth six hundred and fifty!" exclaimed Samuel *Down-Pillow* Sinclair; a fat banker whose tinkering with people's accounts eventually necessitated his involvement with unlawful characters to such a degree, that he was forced to flee his excessively profitable business in a hurry. He did however bring with his immediate baggage a down pillow — an absolute essential for escape.

The Winchester repeated its clap and Samuel Sinclair was

shot in the chest, and he wheezed for a great deal of time, because it seemed his fat had insulated him both from the cold and the instant effects of the bullet. He died over the course of many minutes, and all throughout the remaining exchanges the men around him had to speak up to be heard above the air scraping in and out of his perforated chest.

"I know for a fact he isn't worth that much," Crooked declared. "Might get enough blubber off of him to make a profit, but I'm not lugging him back to civilization to sell as whale-meat."

One of the remaining convicts snickered, Malcolm Murphy.

"How about you, pretty boy?" Crooked asked Murphy. "How much money am I wasting with this next bullet? What would your head fetch?"

"Two hundred sixty dollars."

Crooked paused. "What's your crime?" He cocked his rifle suggesting that lies were no more welcome now than they were before.

"Too many eyes and too few pretty girls."

"Cousins?"

"No, never!"

"Neighbors?"

"Mhmm."

"Got her pregnant?"

"I doubt it."

"Why's that?"

Murphy snickered. "I got there before she was pregnant-age."

Crooked shot him. In the groin. Malcolm screamed loudly enough that the storm gusted in an attempt to spare witnesses their ears. When the wind died and Malcolm had to take a breath,

Crooked pronounced, "You can love women, but not little girls. But that's something for the rest of us to remember, not for you." Crooked shot Malcolm in the face and the clearing was instantly quieter. Someone, somewhere, took a long time hocking, then spat what sounded like a very wet wad of phlegm.

"Get some whiskey, clear your throat, man!" Crooked called. "Or at least have the decency to fire your pistol while you're relocating a lung into your mouth, good Lord! All right, last one… what'd you do and what's your price?"

Crooked cocked his Winchester in preparation and Tim Adams mumbled something to the effect of "Might as well just shoot me."

"And why's that? Speak up!"

"I'm worth less than the others, by a fair bit I reckon."

"Go on."

"I'm a runaway slave. I dunno if they plan to hang me for my crimes or send me back so I can get hung in Mississippi for running away in the first place. Might as well save a whole lot of trouble, just shoot me here."

This time Crooked spat. "I ain't into sob stories. Everyone's got one. But you see my good man Hugo there? Well, he's a coupla shades darker than you are, so I'm perfectly fine employing anyone of any color. But not if they aren't useful. Now, don't give me any more whining. You ran away. Fine. What's your crime? The one you mentioned."

"Rustling pigs."

"Excuse me?"

"Rustling pigs," Tim persisted.

"Are you mispronouncing cattle or are you simple?"

Tim didn't answer.

"Speak up. It's cold, these boys are probably ready for some coffee and hooch, and Lord knows Hugo hasn't had his hand in his pants for long enough."

The bandits laughed.

"Now tell me right this minute, what in the name of our Lord do you mean by rustling pigs?"

"I came up on a farm, no money, not a thing in the world except shoes I stole off a back porch when someone left 'em out to air. These coats are all from dead prisoners who didn't make it. The clothes came from all the same man, he was already wounded though—"

"Tim, I'm cold and growing tired, tell me right this minute what happened."

"Well, I snuck across the farm at night hoping to grab some grub, sneak in the kitchen maybe or something. House was all lit up, people still awake, so I waited in the barn, and they had five big fat pigs just sitting there, sound asleep. I didn't know what a pig fetched, still don't, but I figured they had to be worth something if these people bothered to keep them in a barn with a roof over their head. Anyways, I got a broom off the wall and snuck into the stall then started shooing them out. They were reluctant at first, but then once they got going, I couldn't get any direction from any of them — they just ran around and started squealing. So, I snatched up a little shoat and ran for it but soon I dropped it and they caught me anyways 'cause I couldn't get far, so here I am."

"And what's your bounty?"

"I couldn't read it but they told me it was the lowest so if Garvey's was a hundred mine's less than a hundred."

"Get up Tim. Somebody get him a cigarette and grab up a coat that isn't too bloody. You've been straight with me this whole time; you're coming with us."

Tim wept with joy and thanked Crooked profusely and cried for never having been worth anything to anyone. Crooked told him to get off from his leg, and when Tim turned, wiping grateful tears from his cheeks, Crooked shot him in the back of the head and sent him tumbling face-first in a gory mess into the snow.

Crooked Taylor rode his massive black gelding through the skirling drifts and led his men back into the trees and left their barbarism to the wind and the snow.

Even with his adversaries gone, Mark lay frozen to his spot for quite some time. He tucked his hands away and wiggled his toes as best he could in his boots, but his feet felt wooden to the ankle and his lip was beginning to harden as the wound simultaneously congealed and froze in the winter air.

Mark visited Cigarillo's body, confirmed the knife wound, and imprinted the picture of his friend's last moments into sleepless memory forever. None of the other rangers were faking their deaths as he had been either, and the only horses remaining were those too dead or injured to remove themselves from the clearing.

Mark stumbled through the snow, backtracking their own trail for as long as there was one, until the sun set and there was nothing but the swirling white flakes buzzing in his face like gnats, and the infinite darkness beyond. The wind remained sharp until Mark abandoned the thin whisper of their old horse trail, cutting through thick, whipping pines, seeking refuge in the lee of the mountain's shoulder. The snowdrifts were deep between the trees, and Mark's boots were full to their tops with cold crystals, while he churned his numb legs through soft, relentless dunes that shifted and blew in his face.

The wind's death seemed a miracle, and it came when Mark

mounted a bare spine of stone, and rolled four complete turns, tumbling down the other side of the embankment. The wind still howled, but its razor breath shook the pine trees up above Mark while he wallowed in the sanctuary of this small, heaven-sent depression in the mountain. Mark hunted the valley for brush but found none, and his legs were wooden to the knee and his fingers block-like and useless. Despite the temptation to remain, his only option was to continue to move.

The wind resumed but lacked the ferocity of earlier, and wolf song rang from high up on the mountain. Mark tried not to imagine Cigarillo in a snowdrift, his face horrified and eyes fully open as they waited for his body to be found.

The necessity of movement kept the darkest of the thoughts at bay, and Mark trudged further south across this unexplored face of the mountain until, in answer to a night's worth of prayers, the sun arose and shouldered its way through the snow clouds to offer some sunshine by midmorning.

Mark continued to descend the mountain until the warmth of the day was enough to cause some of the pines to start sweating away their snow. He selected a bare stone stretch on which to sit and stripped off his boots and socks. The tips of his third, fourth and fifth toes looked like they had been dipped in ink. He poked them experimentally with his fingernail, as well as the tip of his small boot knife, but no sensation reached him whatsoever.

"Leave it for the surgeon, Mark," he warned himself. The thawing also meant the wound in his back was less numb, and Mark was optimistic about it until, after laying in the sun for some minutes, he tried to move, and the stiff muscles howled murder at the attempt.

Mark cursed and spit and gnashed his teeth until he was on his feet, and when the stars cleared from his eyes he began to walk again and did so for ten minutes before a beautiful mountain stream burbled across his path. He fell to his knees and realized that his mouth was parched. It was an effort to bend down to the water, but Mark got to his knees and drank until the roof of his mouth was frozen and made his head feel as though it would split. The position on his knees was uncomfortable, so he took one more mouthful of clear mountain runoff, then battled his way to his feet, and continued his journey.

The day was one of intermittent travel, spelled by frequent rest, and constant suffering. The parts of Mark's feet with sensation burned as though they were submerged in a hot spring, and Mark's legs ached and the pain from the wound in his back rose in dizzying torrents, commonly forcing Mark to lean against a tree and close his eyes until the worst had passed.

By sundown the forest promised no refuge, but, too weary for another night of travel, Mark made camp early, collecting an inadequate amount of fallen boughs, then forcing a fire after sufficient effort and cursing were applied to his flint. As soon as the orange flame had been nursed to a size it could sustain, Mark lay down and slept deeply.

He woke in the night and the forest was alive with noise. Perhaps the total darkness created by the clouds scudding across the sky were responsible for an increased acuity in Mark's hearing, but the wind was alive and active, and its gusts pranced among heavy boughs stooped with snow. A heaviness had descended upon Mark, one whose comfortable invitation meant his sleep had allowed him to become too cold. In fact, the night did not feel cold at all but rather pleasant. Mark dabbed his neck and felt nothing in either his fingers or the skin he palpated. He lay back down and pondered staying where he was, but the thought of leaving another body for the wolves — this one especially — caused Mark to rise to his feet and fight the urge to die.

A snowstorm had descended while he slept, but luckily the direction of Mark's staggering march caused him to encounter a wagon train. The wagoners had gotten lost and were similarly caught off-guard by this sudden assault of the snow.

When Mark arrived the wagoners were fighting the tarps that had ripped loose from their wagons, chasing them down and wrestling them into submission so they could stake them into the ground beneath the snow and create some semblance of shelter to stand against the wind. In their haste and the half-lit chaos of activity, the wagoners mistook Mark as one of their own members as he approached, and Mark was handed a shovel and directed to dig out the snow from beneath a wagon so they could tarp-off the wind and take shelter underneath. He numbly worked his hands, tossing spadefuls of snow aside, hoping the wagoners wouldn't notice their mistake for long enough that they might keep him the evening.

The blizzard raged without restraint, and soon forced the wagoners beneath their wagons. The tarp beat like hummingbird wings at the wagon's windward side, and beneath the wagon the gale of the night was muffled somewhat, and there was no illumination at all.

The first light were the embers of cigarettes, appearing one after the next, until a coal lamp flared to life in the center of the claustrophobic space. The cigarette and lamp smoke failed to mask the odor of the wagoners, but when a cigarette was offered to Mark, he took it with a grunt of thanks, and smoked it as nonchalantly as he could.

Sequestered in the half-dark, the men began to talk, and when one elbowed Mark and said, "Eh Clayton?" and from across the huddled circle Clayton responded, "Naw, I'm here."

The man next to Mark said, "Oh, who is it here?"

"Mark."

"Mark?"

"Mark."

"Appleton?"

"Appleton's not here."

"He's the only Mark I know."

"Well, he ain't here."

"Then who is here?"

"Who's Mark?"

"My name is Lieutenant Sinaloa—"

"You a Mexican?"

"A Mexican snuck in under our wagon!"

The lantern was kicked as the men frenzied in the small space to try and subdue Mark, and Mark kicked at someone then crawled toward the windy side of the tent and tossed aside the baggage weighing it down in an attempt to escape.

The tarp collapsed inward, weakened from Mark's wild rearranging, and snow began to rush and pile into Mark's face, blinding him, while he thrashed his legs free of the grip someone had taken on them. The wind was truly fearsome, facing broadside and funneled into that low cavern, and the men hollered for the baggage to be replaced, and Mark sensed opportunity by scrambling onto the tarp himself, his body weight weighing it down to shut out the wind.

"I got it! I got it!" Mark called.

"Where's that dirty Mark?"

"I'm Mark and I've got the canvas!" Mark threatened. "And if anyone comes any closer, I'm going to cut this tarp to ribbons, and we can all have fun freezing to death!"

Mark retrieved his knife and held it near the tarp like a hostage while he calmly explained his reason for appearing so suddenly. With calmer heads the men quickly became sympathetic to Mark's plight, as they themselves had elected to travel in a long wagon train with many members, for fear of being robbed by just the man that Mark was half-sure he had encountered himself.

"Oh, that's Crooked all right," a wagoner named Jon Gray said to the re-formed group; everyone was laying on their bellies, all facing the single lantern again; luckily the lantern had not broken.

"Encountered him m'self, travelling the Arkansas River. This was afore I's travelling with alla these fine folks, just me an' Henry. That's m'gun, Henry, cause it's a 'ol Henry. Heavy, sure, but I don't trust those new Winchesties. Travellin' south, me an' Henry, so jus' one room I paid for a course the rare times I did, mostly one million stars on m'ceiling every night, 'cept when the mist was up, like silver cloth laid down along the river. Then the stars numbered but five, I dunno my consultations though. Not much to do at night cause a million stars is beautiful an all but you kin only look at it fer so long. Man ain't no good at appreciatin' those big things, not for long periods anyways. We played cards. This little fella, hobbling around on canes attached to each arm with rawhide, never drops 'em, tied to his elbows. One time, leanin' against the railin' he just stood there, calm as a clam even though the jeans don't hide that when he was born, he probably came leg first and they were none too gentle with the clampers. But the legs didn't seem to hurt him an' he just stood and smoked an' leaned against the railin' an' let his canes fall, then snapped his arm, quick like this, then caught 'em up again.

Over an' over he did it, a habit, jus' like chewin' grass or whittling for us."

"We played cards—"

"We?"

"Yessir, alla us on the steamer, riding 'long the Arkansas."

"Gray, you never mentioned no steamer."

"How'm I travellin' the river? Struttin' up an' down the waves like Christ himself?"

"Don't be sayin' no blasphemies."

"Let Jon finish his story!"

"Yeah right, thanks!" Silence reigned, and Jon drew deeply on the final butt of his cigarette, then snubbed it in the snow in front of him.

"Us on the steamer played cards 'stead of counting stars. Countin' aces more like — rarer, hah!"

"Jon!"

"Yup. Any which way, in cards he loses — the short fella with the bad legs is none too good of a card player, played too angry, too much emotion. But he talked the whole time an' fooled a good bunch of 'em but not one fella. This guy chewed him up an' spit him out an' when he took Twisty—"

"Crooked."

"Yessum, when he took Crooked all-in an' won, Crooked looked none too pleased. However, to his credit he paid, he'd lost afore an' the men all got paid afore he left the table. He was in his wallet an' the man joked an' said 'you ain't all out, we can play fer yer sticks, or maybe yer legs even — it's not like they're so useful to you now, you kin afford to risk 'em'. He was drunk at this point, and the short fella Crooked had ribbed and taken it just as well as anyone, but this fella took it too far an' we all knew it. 'cept Crooked didn't do nothin'. Not a dern thing all the rest of the trip an' we all wondered why not? He wasn't so fearsome people thought about him an' talked about him during snowstorms under their wagon train, but he had enough reputation at least for his duelin', thought he'd ask the fella up on deck. Didn't do a thing though. Next night we get a card game goin, an' Crooked joins in an' makes no fuss when the insulter, Baker, Bradley, Barnum? Anyways, Baker, no fuss when he joins in it too.

"Cards felt normal, 'ccept Crooked never played Baker a hand. He'd fold, an' it got so obvious someone at the table just had to ask him why. 'I do not want to acum'late no more debt between us' he said. Crooked said, very serious an' talkin' like someone pretty educated, 'Where you gettin' off the boat?'

"I don't remember where he said, but Baker got real nervous wondering why Crooked might wanna follow him off the boat. He even tried to ask one time when he wasn't drunk but Crooked smiled an' said they'd settle everythin' on shore.

"We all watched Baker and he was so unpredictable, I sat with my finger looped in the trigger of my pistol for pretty near three days straight. At the beginning of the trip, men were walkin' around on deck in their long underwear in the middle of the day. Not an Indian or woman or Mexican or robber far as the eye could see, so we all sat easy, and nobody was armed a'tall. After that card game, men looked like they was expectin' to be attacked in hostile country at any moment. I spent some time in hostile country. Not a soldier or ranger or nothin', jus' huntin' pelts out in the territories. You only need to come across one white man skinned, boiled alive and nailed to a tree to fancy sleeping with your pistol loaded. Bein' alone made it so much worse because when the woods is alive an' yer only protection, sleep is the enemy, but it claims to be yer greatest ally, an' every time I blinked, I'd asked myself if I caught enough rest to keep my eyes open until the next moment, I felt safe enough to catch a wink. I slept in the trees, when I wasn't out on the plains where there is no trees a'course. Tied myself up there around the chest each night an' figured if I looked like I was propped up an' waitin' then maybe I'd get killed with arrows fired up instead of captured. Also, it's harder to scale a tree quietly than to walk up on somebody, but I expect if anyone could do it it'd be the Indians; they got footsteps quiet as bat wings flapping.

"So, our boat was armed to the gills an' nobody aboard was none too happy but Crooked didn't give nobody no trouble an' not even nothin' so mean as a hard look. Just a calm collected customer. He had looked angry at the table for murder but, I dunno where he got the control afterwards. I can't imagine a man who'd hear something they're so sore about an' not lose it, but the scary thing about Crooked is that he sees bigger than most men. The whole picture. He followed Baker off the boat, they unloaded both in Howard Harbor, in Nebraska there, though I'm pretty sure I remember correctly Baker said he'd intended to go all the way to Galveston so's he'd need to stay on a piece more if'n he wanted to meet up with the Mississippi. I think maybe he got off when he did 'cause he jus' wanted to get things settled with Crooked, whatever that might be.

"We was all curious as squirrels too, an' a couple the men begged Captain Ro to hold up a day or two in Howard Harbor. They claimed the trip'd been long an' they needed to blow off steam. Captain Ro liked his schedule, but he also liked his fares, an' when men started thinking that maybe another steamer wouldn't be along in too long, Captain Ro gave 'em a day in the city.

"Baker didn't know where to go. He unloaded an' Crooked

followed him off the boat, haulin' his busted-self down the plank on his sticks like he didn't know how slow an' hard it looked for him. What I heard was Baker chose a nice quick pace to walk away, an' Crooked had no way to follow. Didn't seem like he intended to, he turned at a different street, way off behind Baker, but Howard Harbor wasn't so small a city they couldn't meet up.

"Men never got what they wanted. Baker holed up in a room in a hotel somewhere in town an' Crooked didn't get back on the boat. However, those of us who saw it was so interested we kept ears to the ground for months, asking at every city we stopped at after him. Found a fella who'd been a ranch hand for Baker, because Baker actually owned a small ranch in South Texas an' I guess the purpose for going north had been to see if the going was worth going. Like me he only had the details, since he didn't get the first half of the story, but what had happened this fella said, as I told him, the bitterness was built over cards. Edgar, he was the ranch hand I met lookin' fer work, an' Edgar said the way it all shook out was Crooked showed up with some Indians an' pointed 'em right at the ranch an' had 'em round off every cow, horse, chicken, goat, pig, or barn snake that could be captured, and rode off with 'em into a crazy whooping night. Crooked, in all the kerfuffle, found Baker an' shot him in both his hips, then tipped his hat politely to his missus there in the bedroom, her husband hollerin' all hell, then he rode off.

"Baker never walked again, an' the life he'd known as a rancher was done because both his hips had been busted so bad, he could never sit on a horse again. He went broke, Crooked lined everyone up like prisoners, an' once everyone was safe out the house, they burned it all to the ground. Crooked rode off on Baker's favorite horse an' left Baker with no home, no money, no livestock, an no ability to pull him an' his family up from the dirt.

"Crooked Taylor coulda shot Baker in the head at the card table an' been done with it. A lotta people woulda been saved a lotta pain if he done it that way, but he came after Baker like a plague an made sure he wiped out his whole life, then left him miserable an' broken an' alive to feel all the pain."

At this time, Mark explained, the wagoner Jon Gray had finished his story. As for himself, Mark explained that he had aided the wagoners in their quest back to civilization, and in exchange, a man named Simon Gurley had trimmed off the frostbitten tips of his toes with his buck knife against the flat face of a piece of wood. The toes needed additional care when Mark and the wagon train arrived at Fort Orre, but the doctor was a sympathetic man who agreed to take credit, and Mark would have gladly paid him his due, had his gambling debts in Fort Orre not made a hasty departure from town in the middle of the night necessary.

Three

"I can understand killers, not that I been around very many in my life, by why did Crooked interview the four of 'em? Why not shoot 'em all and be done with it?" Moses Louis-May spat. He wore a straw hat so old its brim afforded Moses little more shade than a spiderweb, and so his face was well on its way to burning. His nose was plum-colored from years in the sun, and the skin looked like the hard crust on a spud potato. Above his nose, two eyes, beady but bright, dared any man to object to his statement.

"Because he ain't like that," Broadstreet informed Moses. Ed gave everyone in the circle a smug look before he continued. "I heard him explain it once. Looked him dead in the eye as he spoke from me to you away. He talked about life and death, and what motivates men to act a certain way."

"No! Really? How'd you come to meet him?" Moses spluttered.

Broadstreet smiled and Joel figured it might be a good time for a smoke, so he patted his jeans for his rolling papers. Mark crossed his arms, canted his head skeptically, and the way the brim of his hat cut the sun it left a wedge of light bisecting his face across the tip of his nose, his awkward mustache, and his dark beard.

"I can't say I had the pleasure of knowing him well, but I feel as though I can brag a bit because I rode in the company of Major Lionel McCleod for a brief time back when Crooked was loose, the most wanted man west of the Mississippi. He made even a couple of real fierce Indian chiefs, Bluefoot and Song of Summer take a back seat to him for a time..."

Like the tip of the spear, Fort Saint Thomas was the most westerly point of civilized Texas. Beyond lay the uncharted wastes owned by the failing Indians; those still fighting against the immense and inevitable takeover of progress.

The horns sounded early, many blasts, urgent and unsympathetic to the shattered quiet. Ed rose from his bunk and the air felt cold on his skin as he drove his legs into his starchy uniform and buttoned his shirt. He was not the last in his hardscrabble outfit to arrive at the parade grounds; the sun was yet to make its appearance, although a pink glow in the east announced that it would not be long in coming.

The parade ground looked like packed salt from the relentless drilling demanded of the men, and visible lines were etched like small furrows in a garden, and it was into these well-worn trails that the men assembled their boots, as Major Lionel McCleod stood at the front with his back to the rising sun. His horse dared not whinny or complain about the lather she had accumulated during his morning ride, for McCleod's entire stable of horses were overworked despite their generous feedings.

McCleod hammered the men into lines by his will. Men's hands fumbled at their buttons, and shirts were checked and re-checked for presentability. Even the men in the back did not feel safe, for it seemed nothing in the outfit was overlooked by McCleod any longer.

The wooden bastions encircling the parade grounds were composed of fresh timber still wearing skins of rough bark, as much of the old fence had been burned, and the timber to replace it had not yet been sand-blasted into smoothness by the prairie wind.

McCleod did not speak. When he was satisfied with the arrangement of the men before him, he nodded toward his lieutenants, and this set the entire operation into motion. McCleod did not permit chaos. He stiffly oversaw the assembly of his units; the action was swift, and no man dawdled. A fresh horse was brought to him, and the gates opened wordlessly. McCleod mounted and rode out of Fort Saint Thomas headed west, with every confidence that his battalion would follow.

The wind picked up along the rise, but Ed appreciated it's coolness brushing the sweat stains beneath his arms. Francis nickered and Ed agreed, and he eased the pace to a gentle trot. When Ed crested the hill, he looked out across a vacant plain, as formless as the one they had camped on for the past ten days. The sun was so hot it shone white, and the land was beaten yellow and shade-less. Nothing but scratchy chaparral could stand any higher than the top of a man's boot. A flat ocean of sand built for rattlesnakes, not for men.

Ed turned and considered riding back to the battalion, but his horse Francis had suffered greatly all afternoon, and with nothing to report he took a careful swig of water and swished it thoroughly, wishing he could spit it from his mouth, warm and gritty as it was. But he swallowed it and closed his eyes for a moment…

"What's this got to do with him shooting people in the snow?" Moses interrupted.

"Because he told me once, to my face all about life and death—"

"I know, you said so already, I heard you. But what's that

gotta do with him interviewing and then shootin' everybody?"

"I was going to talk about the battle of Gila Flats; I was a private with Lieutenant Schneider—"

"The hell has that got to do with what I'm saying?" Moses snapped, his voice becoming higher and more strung-out with each repetition of his question.

"Just tell him that part," Joel suggested.

"I thought—"

"Can somebody answer my darn question?"

"He does it because—"

"Here, I'll tell it," Ed snapped at Joel.

"He doesn't want the long version."

"I'll tell it short."

"Somebody God-dang tell it!"

"Watch yer language, there's ladies present!" A rough man in overalls spat tobacco from his rotten lower lip, disgusted that Moses and company would employ such vulgar profanities so freely. He nodded toward a woman who was trying to prevent a brood of six young children from terrorizing the chickens that were pecking for food in the dooryard out front of the church.

"All right, all right," Ed said, holding his hands up and relenting. "All right. So, in the case of the prisoners up in the mountains—"

Before tensions could rise any higher, the church doors were thrown open and Jasper Calafort boomed out with a baritone like cannon fire, "People! Our great savior, the worthy Christian Lionel McCleod is being called by the Lord to return to his kingdom! Let us pray together that his passage may be painless, and that our earthly lives be lived well, forever keeping his sacrifice in our hearts!"

No member of the crowd could avert their attention from

Jasper's magnetic sermon, and even Ed (interrupted once again) cursed under his breath only once before joining into the prayer *Our Father*, led emphatically by Jasper Calafort, perched and posing like a prophet atop the stone steps of the church.

"Sons and daughters of the Lord!" Jasper hollered. "This great man, he who sacrificed his flesh for ours may not awaken again. The doctors have done all they can, but it seems as though his time on this earth may be ending. Those who wish to speak with him, to send his soul with kind wishes as it departs most assuredly for heaven, come to me. I will lead you in his last rites and we will all sing so gloriously, the Lord our God will have no choice but to hear us and direct his attention upon our deliverer!"

The crowd surged like water into a funnel, and even Jasper, sturdy oak of a man that he was, stepped hesitantly backward as the crush of the churchyard approached him on the steps.

"Patience! Patience my sons and daughters! Do not kick and punch one another for a place in line! Conduct yourselves as Christian men and women and be civil or there will be no entry into my church!"

Jasper's great voice held the crowd from entering the church but could not dissuade their violence. A mendicant reeking of hooch claimed he was a relative of McCleod's, and he pulled a knife and wet the dusty churchyard with blood as he shouted drunkenly that he would not be shoved again. A pistol was fired into the air as someone called for order, but some men who had been brawling took this as a sign of escalation, and, fearful that it was one of their enemies that had brought guns to what had been a fistfight, they began to draw arms.

"The Lord will permit no lead to fly on this day of mourning! The next heathen to pull a trigger can answer to the Lord himself!" Jasper, having retreated inside the doors of the church, re-emerged with a 10-gauge shotgun whose barrel had been hacked short, augmenting it into a handheld cannon. The ferocity with which Jasper Calafort reentered the scene captured enough of the mob's attention that the majority of the gunfire subsided. One man lay dead in the street, and no one tended to him because he had no head left above the brow of his hat. Another man sat propped against a low fence that had been bent during the scuffle, and some men were offering him canteens and cigarettes, allowing him to drink and smoke his fill before he passed on.

"If you are wounded kindly move to the side! Sister Abigail will be out to tend to you!" Calafort boomed. "Uninjured persons, line up! I will lead thee into the room of our savior, however, you will be respectful and reverent, or I will remove you!" The callused hands dwarfing the sawed-off shotgun suggested that the removal of most any person would be no great effort for the priest. On the whole the crowd obeyed, and the keeper of their hero slowly admitted those who had been lucky enough to make the front of the line without injury.

The mendicant that had claimed relation to Major McCleod ended up being the man missing the majority of his hat and skull, and his pockets were emptied, the bag he had with him went missing, but otherwise the body was left where it fell. Those not yet entering the church stood in line and continued to smoke and drink and converse.

Four

Major Lionel McCleod lay on a bed that had been brought into the cloister of the church for him. The bed huddled against the wall where sunbeams darting through the old boards lit the billows of smoke rising continually from the long pipe Doctor Chen smoked. Like a train, he failed to operate without chuffing exhalations, and he stepped back from his patient and sighed through his nostrils; you could tell by the tusks of smoke attached there for a moment.

"No good. The hole still cries blood." Doctor Chen shook his head and Sister Abigail tipped her flask up and nodded her head in agreement.

"Has our lion awakened?" Jasper inquired.

"No. No words. Just 'huh, huh'," Doctor Chen said, imitating the pained breathing of McCleod.

"How many shots was it?"

Jasper whirled upon the crowd of men craning in the door.

"Who asked that?"

There was no answer.

"Who asked it?"

Jasper approached the men and stood a head taller than all of them, and when he extended his thick arms across the doorway and told the men none of them were entering until the blasphemer was identified, they believed him. "You will not move an inch until the man is pointed out. And..." Jasper said, pausing to let his glare have its effect upon the men, "...for those protecting him, know that our angel Major McCleod is dying with none but drunk Sister Abigail to comfort him—"

"I ain't drunk. You cain't get drunk afore noon!" Sister Abigail squawked.

"Some men are injured in the courtyard, go tend to them," Jasper said.

"Should I bring the doctor too? See if his miracles work on some easier patients? I bet he can cure a hangnail up real good, that Chinese—"

"Sister, enough!" Jasper snapped.

She drowned her complaint with a gurgle from her flask and exited, barefooted, her heels rasping like boot leather on the church's dirt floor.

"It ain't done."

In the silence of the hot cloister of the church, Major McCleod choked out his first words since stumbling into Aspirations Texas alone, injured, and on-foot.

Jasper and the men left the door and flew to McCleod's side, and his eyes remained closed, but he moaned again. "It ain't done." He was shirtless and the sheet covered him below the arms, but a small red blossom had seeped through his bandage and the white sheet fabric both.

"What ain't done?" Curtis Todd asked.

"He isn't," Jasper declared. "He is regaining his strength! He is pronouncing that he will throw off the shackles of death itself!"

McCleod moaned again, but it was unintelligible, and the great enthusiasm and encouragement he received from his visitors did not call forth any more words.

"Is he going to make it, or do we say our prayers?" Jasper asked, leaning against the wall to confer with Doctor Chen.

"He won't make it. Maybe today, maybe tomorrow. He won't make it long."

Jasper nodded and patted the doctor then returned to the small, hopeful group.

Five

The sun had grown hot, and shadows were scarce as it hung almost directly overhead. Ed Broadstreet wiped sweat from his nose and switched the foot he was standing on, at the bottom of the church steps. But as the first of the churchgoers to see Major McCleod exited the rear of the church, they did so in a rowdy procession, causing every head in the waiting line to turn toward the mob, looping around the back of the church toward Main Street. Ed noticed men peeling away from their wives to go find good central seats in the saloons, where gossip could be most easily acquired. The line was eager and at the threshold people had once more abandoned their manners, squeezing and shoving past one another to gain another inch toward their goal. It amazed Ed that such a rambunctious horde could so quickly transform into reverent, God-fearing people for the brief period they stood within the walls of the church and paid their respects to the dying McCleod. But as these same people exited the rear of the church, they stuffed their hats back down onto their heads and ran gleefully toward the devil's gallery of the outside world where they could resume their madness.

The air grew denser as the line approached their dying saint, thick with exhaled smoke and the dust that drifted like mist off of people's clothing. As Ed entered the shade of the church he heard a hacking cough, followed by a disgusting harumph of wet phlegm, then a juicy, Adam's-apple bobbing swallow. He turned and saw Moses Louis-May not two people behind him in line, his hat against his chest and his sunburnt eyelids closed as he mumbled in prayer.

Ed scowled. The line inched forward, and Ed wondered how he, a man who had served under Major McCleod, should be made to stand in line with farmers, mule-men and thugs, but he did not voice this opinion aloud.

When Ed entered the cloister, he could sense his proximity to their fading angel by how quiet the room had become. Only Jasper Calafort could be heard, his normally booming voice constrained to a mouse's whisper as he passed from person to person.

"I'm sorry for your mourning, my son, did you know the deceased?" Ed nodded at Jasper and tried to look around him, but the room was too small and the man too large. "I rode with him, or, under one of his lieutenants. Once."

"I am glad to hear it. However, you notice the church is in great disrepair. We have been taking care of Major McCleod, just Sister Abigail and myself, and, with Crooked just recently dispatched, we have not yet had any new shipments of food. Sister Abigail and myself have gladly been giving up our portions, but food is scarce and any charity you have will be blessed tenfold in the eyes of the Lord for being bestowed upon those who have suffered and sorely need it." Jasper smiled and Ed tried not to show his billfold to Jasper as he produced a banknote of one dollar; peeling it free from the rest.

"Here. And, you let me know if there's anything I can do to help. You've done good work taking care of Major McCleod, making him comfortable in his final hours."

Jasper took the note and bowed and mouthed 'thank you' emphatically but without making a sound, before he turned and put a gentle hand on the man behind Ed. Someone in front wept quietly, but too many people had stopped around the deathbed of the major for Ed to see who it was. Ed looked around and saw Moses Louis-May wave Jasper away without making a donation, and Ed turned back toward the line and scowled again.

When Ed reached Major McCleod he realized he had nothing to say. But he consoled himself since the man lying in front of him was near-enough to a corpse that there was nothing he could say that the man would hear anyways. Ed decided to keep it simple, thinking that it would look worse trying to be a hero and stumbling, than simply saying a couple of words that were true.

"I uh, I didn't know you well, but you were an honorable man and I was proud of the time I spent fighting in your unit. I hope you—"

McCleod's face was as white as the belly of a trout, but when his eyes fluttered open, they blazed with life and Ed could not help but react, gasping in surprise, along with two or three others.

"He's waking up!"

"It's not done!" McCleod wheezed.

The crowd began to get excited, voices stirring like a hive of bees becoming angry, but Jasper was the first to act. He was standing near a lowly widow, holding out the wallet she had sewn from some old boots for the major, as her donation and parting gift, and Calafort took and stuffed the wallet into his robe then waded into the crowd and shoved his way to the bedside of Major McCleod.

"Quiet everyone! Not a sound!"

"Crooked's out there," McCleod wheezed. His eyes were mostly white and rolled wildly like those of a spooked horse, but they found Ed and locked onto him, and Ed felt the strings of his guts tighten as Major McCleod spoke to him. "I got him but he ain't finished. Backtrack my trail and finish it."

"Where've you been? Round here? I know all these parts like the back of my hand, been herding cattle to and fro since I was a toddler!" Moses Louis-May announced.

"He's armed and dangerous, I'm a former soldier," Ed intervened.

Excitement took hold of the men again, but this time Jasper did not possess the power of personality to curb their lust for action. The men spilled from the church, hollering their message, and soon the wild noise of a gathering posse took grip of Aspirations and began to shake it, every citizen in a drunken frenzy over the renewed hunt for Crooked Taylor.

Six

The wild stampede of men exited the church, hollering for their horses if they had comrades to fetch them, or else just pumping their arms while they ran, keeping their gaze low so as not to trip on a youngster, or the hitch of a poorly parked wagon.

One sunburnt man mounted his horse in the square and spurred it while he shot his pistol, prompting the horse to buck him. His head cushioned most of his fall, but since he was awake by the time Sister Abigail got to him, and since there were a number of other fools in greater need than he was, she did nothing more than scoot the sunburned man out of the way from being trampled.

Except for a select few, the majority of the mob mounted their horses with more success, but Ed Broadstreet did not follow the stream of excited citizens. Broadstreet remained inside the church, walking in the wake of Jasper Calafort as the priest strode down a hallway filled with drifting dust motes, leading to his humble room.

"They know how far they're riding?" Ed asked as Father Calafort opened the door and stepped into his room. With the way Father Calafort had to stoop, Ed doubted the room had room for two, so he crossed his legs and leaned against the wall in the hallway.

"Doubt it," Calafort said. For once he was neither talkative, nor smiling, and instead he seemed intent on rummaging through a great number of papers and books. Ed found the volume of books odd as he figured there was only one Bible to know, but, recognizing that he had not read the book himself, he figured he might be unaware of it being a multi-part series, or one that required learning that extended beyond just those pages.

Ed watched Calafort toss his sawed-off 10-gauge onto his cot. He leaned further into the room, and from the shadows produced a serape that had been hung on the wall.

"Got any saddlebags?" Ed asked Father Calafort.

"I don't have a horse."

"I'll outfit you." Ed turned and Moses Louis-May stood in the hallway behind him, a wad of tobacco bulging his cheek as he grinned.

"You shouldn't be going, old-timer," Ed said.

"You know where to water your horse at? You know when to slow up because of hidden arroyos and gulches? You'll ride off a ridge 'n' break yer neck without me." Moses, forgetting himself, leaned to spit, but he halted this at the last moment and looked about frantically while Ed chuckled.

Moses sneered as he sucked for breath through his nose, then, staring Ed in the eye, he swallowed what he had intended to spit, and held his face strict enough that from a distance it looked as though he had tolerated it well.

"Forgets his manners and his spittoon, how can we expect to survive without him?" Ed sneered.

"We?" Father Calafort asked, folding a spare set of clothes into his serape, along with a hunk of bacon wrapped in paper, a wedge of cheese, and a sack of dried beans. He compartmentalized each item with expert folding, then slung the whole package around one shoulder in a tidy bundle.

"Of course, we. I was a soldier; I rode with him—"

"What've you done lately?" Moses coughed. He was green

at the gills and leaning precariously against the wall outside Father Calafort's room, but he had not yet stepped outside.

Ed nodded back down the hallway toward the cloister where McCleod lay, attended by some old men who had not rushed out. "If Major McCleod came back in that bad of shape and he's waking up scared that Crooked's still out there, I say an experienced soldier would be of great value to this outfit."

Jasper nodded and turned to address Moses, but the old man was scuttling away, heaving as he tried to fight the convulsions and hold in his vomit with his fingers.

"I never should've let this mob inside," Father Calafort said. He shut the door to his room and locked it, then walked back toward the cloister, Ed dropping in behind to follow him once more.

Moses' path was traceable from where his vomit had started to spill, but his path led outside to the left through the door, but Jasper and Ed turned right and stopped off at the cloister so Jasper could poke his head inside.

"Simmons, Kirk, you two in there?" he called.

"Rollie too!" a hacking voice responded.

"Don't get too drunk, and don't let Sister Abigail get too drunk, and don't let McCleod die, and don't let any of those boys outside bleed out or cook to death in the sun. Raid the pantry as much as you need. It's pretty much empty but treat it as your own."

"Yessir Padre, we're on it!"

"Is McCleod still awake?" Calafort waited for a response but whoever had been answering lapsed into giggles until Calafort stepped fully into the room. "Simmons," Calafort snapped, summoning quiet sobriety from the men. "Is McCleod still awake?"

"No. Back to sleeping. No moaning no nothing, just light breathing."

"I mean it, Simmons, tend to him."

"You know me, Father, I kid but I always get the job done."

"Except when you don't. See, that this one gets done." With this, Jasper Calafort left the men in the cloister and walked to the front of the church, Ed following behind him.

When they arrived at the front of the church, the two of them were met by Moses Louis-May, whose complexion was green but face tight and determined.

"You're not coming, Moses," Ed growled.

"Shuttit. It's my horses we're using."

"We don't need an old horse-hand getting himself shot."

"Mind your own hide, you ain't nothin' but a retired soldier that don't know where he's headed."

"Stop this nonsense, we need you both," Calafort said. "That posse up ahead is useless. They're all drunk and they're going to burn their horses out by sunset. We'll catch up with their camp tomorrow and the hungover ones will be heading the other way because they'll have figured out how useless that charge was." Calafort looked from one man to the other and back again, but neither had any words to interject. "I'm glad you two had level enough heads not to lope off. I expect some others might come equipped too, and like you said, Ed, we don't know what condition Crooked is in, or who was with him. I'm not going to get into it now, but McCleod took off after him, armed, and on a good, trusty horse. He barely made it back and is in mortal condition. We don't know the trouble we're running toward." Calafort's talk stifled the bickering between Moses and Ed and replaced it with an ominous silence. "I'm going to go get water and, Moses, if the offer still stands, pick out a horse of yours that's sturdy enough for hard travel."

"I meant every word, we'll get situated," Moses said.

"I have my own horse and gear," Ed volunteered.

"Good," Moses said.

"Let's meet back in an hour. Pack only the essentials, we'll have to ride fast," said Calafort.

Ed and Moses nodded in agreement. Moses headed off with Calafort, and Ed headed back down the main street toward the hotel he was staying in.

Seven

The horses grunted, whinnied, and nipped one another, and were nearly as rambunctious as the men that rode them. The horses travelled in a dense mob and swam chest-deep through the dust of those in front, all the while jockeying for position down the main avenue of Aspirations.

As the last clapboard structures of the town dropped behind the racing pack, the herd began to stretch out, the pacing horses with wind in their sails navigating toward the periphery where they could chew up chunks of flat desert with ease, leaving the horses with short, ugly, mule-trot strides to struggle stubbornly in their wake.

However, not every rider appreciated the reality of their steeds, and Bucky Gardiner had taken to the drink to such a point that he refused to believe in his position toward the rear of the pack. The amazing fact that his mule was ahead of some through-and-through horses, and a good five hands shorter than any other creature loping across the seared plains, did not spare the mule from Bucky's quirt. Predictably, when the mule grew tired of its treatment it refused to run any longer, and so Bucky made the mistake of stepping down off the mule and presenting a target for its torment. Bucky got off one good strike before the mule reared up like a horse and pawed the air, catching Bucky in the mouth with a hoof. Bucky spun free of a mouthful of his teeth and dropped to the dust. His mule landed atop him and pawed his shoulder blade hard for good measure, but when it tried to walk off, unconscious Bucky's wrist was still looped in its reins. The mule pulled Bucky face-down for a few feet, but its exhaustion was too great to continue. It attempted to graze among the ash-bare desert and came away nibbling some stringy gray stalks of grass.

Most men made off with superior luck to Bucky, but the herd tore like a disorganized dust-devil across the plains, shedding equipment, and every so often a rider.

Mark had had his eye on Michael Lougheed for quite some time. Lougheed had brandished a pretty mare Mark fancied while drinking at the hotel's saloon, and his watch and his boots and his fine collection of hats made Mark follow behind him when Lougheed made a fool of himself back in Aspirations, missing the stirrup, and nearly planting his face in the street. His wife recommended he sleep it off, or at least drink some coffee and catch up with the men, but in Mark's humble opinion Lougheed had no more appreciation for fine headwear than he did for fine women. He chastised his pretty wife more coarsely than Mark felt any lady should hear in public, so when Lougheed wobbled atop his mount, Mark guessed that the sun had reached its crucial point, interacting with his inebriation and the fatigue of riding.

Mark rode up on Lougheed's left, and the man was so comatose in the sun that he did not even react to Mark's approach. Mark reached level with Lougheed, and all it took was one quick push and Lougheed toppled sideways from the saddle. Mark was ready and grabbed the mare's reins. He knew little more about horses than what it felt like to ride a good one versus a bad one, but the saddle and reins and accoutrements spread across the beautiful beast suggested that the animal sporting the gear would match the exorbitant pedigree of its owner's kit. The saddlebags felt heavy, and Mark yearned to root through every pocket and fold in their entirety, and it pained him to leave Lougheed wheezing in the sun when he still wore such fine clothing from head-to-toe; but the horse would have to suffice.

Mark spurred Toledo and felt the reins in his hand tighten, but Lougheed's brown and white mount was agile for its size and receptive to the lead and fell comfortably into rhythm behind Toledo.

"Good horse," Mark said.

By midday riders appeared to the north, and the blistering void between them and Mark sizzled like the top of a skillet. Mark had kept a slow pace all morning, staying well back from the cloud of dust kicked up by the angry column of men. He knew that he shouldn't go trotting his new horse in front of too many pairs of eyes — lest the saddle, the reins, or the animal itself be identified — but the purposeful pace of this new group caused guilty fear to stick like an arrow in Mark's stomach.

He slapped Toledo on the flanks to quicken his pace, and jerked the new horse's reins, signaling that she needed to pick up from her lazy trot as well. "Let's go, enough dawdling. He didn't walk back to Aspirations *that* fast, but we still need to be careful."

Mark rode Toledo and towed his new horse in behind. He swiveled his head every so often, and even loosed his rifle from its scabbard and tried to look through the scope — all this while on the run — to see if he could identify the small group, stubbornly continuing south. He would have liked to cut east some time ago and make his way back up the trail, skipping Aspirations altogether, if possible, but he would be well within sight of this group behind him. Accelerating posed the same problem, where he would catch up with the largest body of the posse that had set out, which still rode in front of him.

"I guess it'll take some wits and some luck both. But you're a lucky horse ain't you?" The stolen horse did not answer the call Mark tossed over his shoulder, and they rode on, Mark unable to travel far before having to look behind him again.

Mark paced it so that he did not catch the main group out in front, but by sundown he could not avoid contact with the group to the north. Nothing screamed 'horse thief' like one man riding two horses in the dark, and so Mark was forced to stop, and he tucked in with a small band of four other men who had made camp on the open plains for the night. Mark decided that guilty men do not join other men for camp.

With a heavy red dusk upon them, Father Calafort, Clarita Louis-May, Moses Louis-May, and Ed Broadstreet rode up to the camp Mark had joined. Mark stood up from the cookfire around which four other men sat, their horses hobbled and grazing in the sparse weeds just beyond the shadows cast by the early fire.

"Father."
"Ed."
"Father."
"Norton."
"Clarita."
"Cal."
"Mark."
"Moses."
"Mooney."
"Sween."
"Father."

"I count six horses, where'd you get the spare?" Calafort asked, snapping off the greetings and looking off into the quickly failing light.

"I picked him up," Mark said. "Found her headed south and all done up but with no rider. Figured one of our posse owns her."

"You check for a brand?"

"Yup."

"Did you find one?"

"Yessir, but not one I'm familiar with."

"Well, you're right I'm sure she's one of ours. All day we came across men on their feet who claimed they left Aspirations on horses." Calafort laughed. "There's going to be a parade of foolish cowboys lurching into Aspirations at all hours of the night. I'm sure any one of them would appreciate a ride. We'll send the spare horse back with the next group passing by that way, it can take one of the men that most needs a ride."

"Smart," Mark said, trying hard to keep his voice level. He stirred the fire with a twig, but the fire needed no tending as it danced its orange dance atop the crackling underbrush.

"You all mind if we join your campsite here? There's not much sunlight left for riding."

"Course, Father!"

"It'd be our pleasure!"

Comments from the other men welcomed Calafort, and so he and his small group dismounted and tended their horses, hobbling them and setting up their own tents for the night.

The sun grew tired, the prairie shadows long, and the great darkness of the limitless heavens constricted the small group around the fire, making them scoot closer and closer until they were all practically side-by-side and touching.

Conversation waxed and waned across topics of hunting and travel and boyhood mischief, until a topic more sinister than all the rest reared its head in the perfect dark.

"Hey, Mark, you ever meet Crooked other than that time in

the mountains?" Mark looked across the fire at Ed who was facing him, sitting barefoot, his sweaty socks mounted on some flat stones in front of the fire. Moses and Clarita had their heads bent together in a whispered argument that was gaining volume, and Father Calafort was pretending he couldn't hear them while he bent his head back and looked up at the stars.

"No, that was it," Mark said, reluctant to re-engage in the topic.

"Lucky you made it out alive," Ed said. His focus was entirely centered upon Mark, and Mark looked away out past the fire at nothing. When his eyes returned, Ed was still staring at him, awaiting his response.

"I agree. It was nothing but luck and luck alone."

"Got any scars?" Mark thought this an odd question, but Ed elaborated. "You said you took a bullet in the face, it saved you from his men, the bleeding I mean."

Mark smiled then lifted his mustache to expose the missing piece of upper lip. "I still talk pretty good because I have the whole right side of my lip. You can see," Mark said, pulling the hair away and extending his mouth sideways. "It tore off the left half of my upper lip and lots of the cheek." Mark laughed at the slight benefit of his disfigurement. "I always smoke out that side and it looks like I do it on purpose, but I just let the smoke out." He laughed again and as the conversation lulled, Ed pounced.

"I met him," Ed said. "Face to face, chatted with him, just the two of us."

Mark could tell that Ed's desire to tell his story was eating him internally, but he was hoping for an early sunset and as little moon as possible tonight.

"Mhmm. Wild stuff. However, I for one am getting pretty tired—"

"You met him?" Moses asked Ed.

Mark sighed and tugged his hat brim in frustration.

"Yessir, I did," Ed pronounced. Mark sensed a lengthy story approaching, and so he made his hasty exit from the campfire's circle.

"My stomach isn't feeling so hot. Think I might call 'er a night." Mark did not wait for comment, but rose and stalked off, away from the fire to where his bedroll lay. He had not pitched his tent because it did not look like rain and the saddlebags were not entirely out of the question. He lay down, closed his eyes, and listened to the chatter coming from around the fire. But the fire was not alone. Across the empty plains were some few orange dots of life, separated by great swaths of night, and each fireside was surrounded by similar conversations; men speaking to one another in hushed voices as though to ward off the enormity of the night.

"I still met him," Ed reminded everyone.

Moses looked at Clarita, but her attention was on the horses. Her buckskin had taken to sniffing the wind, and she ignored her husband until such time as her mount began to relax. At this point she turned to him and wondered why he was looking so starry-eyed in her general direction.

"Huh?"

"Ed said he met Crooked," Moses relayed.

"I know, I heard him."

"You were faced the other way, I was just saying."

"I can look and hear at the same time."

"Well, I didn't know."

"Like I hadn't said so a thousand times before."

"Woman, you are a headache."

"Because I make you use your brain."

"Ahem," Ed coughed, in an attempt to remind the small convent around the fire that he had a story to tell.

"We all know you met him," Clarita snapped at Ed. "Did you kiss him or what? What're you so darn proud of?"

"I'm proud because I lived to tell the tale," Ed defended. "There aren't many men Crooked has set his sights on who escaped, but the wound here in my shoulder..." Ed tugged the collar of his shirt aside and hunched his shoulder toward the gap in the clothing, but in the darkness, it was impossible to see this most cherished physical emblem upon his person. "It's proof that I'm one of the lucky ones..."

Eight

Visiting the post office in Austin, Texas yielded nothing but sorrow for Edward Broadstreet:

Dear Ed, hope Texas is treating you well. I'm in Cinsinatti, Ohio, not doing great myself. They want to hang me for helping runaway slaves across the river even though they paid the toll fare an' square. I tried telling them I didn't know they'd run away but that didn't hold up. Any help would be apreshiated. Your brother, Will.

The letter was heavy in the breast pocket of Ed's shirt, but furlough was over; Ed drank too much that night (trying not to think) and he and the others rode out the next day, departing at dawn, and drawing rein only for necessary relief of their horses, until dusk saw them through the gates of Fort Saint Thomas.

Ed slept from the great fatigue of the day prior, and the next morning saw no relief, as Major Lionel McCleod addressed them all in the parade grounds at dawn. The closest the major came to Ed Broadstreet that day was when he stood at the front of Ed's line, to address the captain of his column, Captain Rainier. Ed remembered that the sun had risen a rosy red, coloring the major like anger, and though Major McCleod looked at Captain Rainier as he spoke, his voice carried across all of the parade grounds. "Captain, your orders are as follows," stated Major McCleod to Captain Rainier. The men in the front rows near the major nearly sweat, their muscles were so taut from standing at attention, but the major's voice was measured even as he delivered his orders. "You will depart from Fort Saint Thomas and head west until you cross the Rincon River, after which point your unit will turn north. You will be entering Comancheria, which is Indian territory. However, your objective is to push north until you encounter either Bradley Taylor, or rendezvous with the northern column led by Captain Venett. The purpose of this expedition is to put an end to Bradley Taylor's lawlessness. Therefore, I expect this order to be the primary and only objective throughout, and for this to be the case for every man present. Bradley Taylor will be brought to me. I do not care if he is alive or dead, only that he is identifiable."

Ed figured all that would be needed to identify Crooked Taylor was his lower half, but neither he nor anyone else would dare voice such a thing in Major McCleod's presence.

On only the second morning out from Fort Saint Thomas they crossed the Rincon River; a drip of a river nearly dry where they rode across, barely wetting the horses past their fetlocks. The troupe was treated to another glorious sunset after an empty afternoon of featureless prairie.

Captain Rainier forbade the men from riding over the tops of the rolling hills, instead demanding his men to wend in between them; he wanted no easy silhouettes against the marble-blue sky, should Crooked and his men be looking. Instead, his eyes and ears came from the two white scouts that, in the opinion of the men, were sent ahead to survey the country far too infrequently.

Often, in a low voice, one man would ask another how big the biggest tribes of Indians were and ponder whether this should be their greater concern. But as the nervous men talked, it was still Crooked Taylor that shone most brightly in their fearful imaginations. The cripple was ferocious no-doubt, but in assembling all of their stories, his deeds became greater than what any man could hope to accomplish. But, with so many claims attributed to the man, some had to at least hold some truth, and so the difficulty became separating fact from fiction. But when neither fact nor fiction could be decided upon, stories were repeated, questioned, and speculation ran wild. Answers were left up to the minds of those who thought that answers could be had.

The light bled out of the world as though some great injury in the west saw the brightness drain from the dying sky. And a long ride full of stories about murder, torture, and narrow escapes from murder and torture resulted in a heartfelt reluctance from every man to be the first to wander out onto the prairie alone and stand watch. Ed felt the reluctance of his colleagues keenly, and therefore had to be careful with how eager he appeared to volunteer for watch.

Ed let Captain Rainier repeat his question twice before he pretended to be reluctant in raising his hand to volunteer. What he had not voiced during the ride to his colleagues, was that for all of their stories and fabricated terror, the letter in his breast pocket meant more to him than chasing crippled ghosts.

When Ed finally did volunteer, Captain Rainier thanked him several times for his initiative. Ed loathed the captain's thankfulness for it suggested remembrance, but his mind had been made up regardless; Ed could not let his own blood drop in Ohio, while he fought on the frontier of Texas, for the safety of people he would never know.

At dusk Sober Ned doled out some extra coffee to Ed and clapped him on the shoulder. Ed nodded to him and turned to eat his meal in solitude. Before the sun had even set many were hunkered in their bedroll, and the horses were no better, exhausted from two days' hard riding.

It pained Ed to leave his bedroll on the ground when he knew he would need it, but he could not ride out of camp with anything that might suggest what he was about to do. When he mounted, the sun had nearly quit the world, already starting to glow on some other hemisphere, as it left this one to darkness.

Captain Rainier approached Ed, and behind him, Ed saw Hank Lacoste frowning toward them both. Perhaps Hank was perturbed because Ed was already mounted and apparently eager to begin his shift, meaning that as the other scout, Hank's time of rest was over too.

"I'm thinking you head a mile out, no more than that," Rainier said. He was a short man but thick through the wrists and fingers and sturdy enough to work like he was large. His hat was low, and he twitched his mustache as the evening shadow pooled in the deep pockmarks of his cheeks. "Wait for the sun to set entirely, then set up on top of that ridge there."

Ed squinted and looked at where Captain Rainier was pointing. "Just that ridge there? I don't know that that's a full mile."

"The next good rise is too far. If you encounter someone, I want to be close enough that we can get to you in time."

"Sure, but if I can't see much further ahead than you can from right here, what good am I scouting?" Ed asked.

Captain Rainier shook his head. "Still. I've thought I was prepared before, and it cost men their lives. I'd rather you be too close than— It's better to be cautious, even though we haven't encountered anyone. That first ridge, and no further. Set yourself up just after dark. We'll scout from here until then."

Captain Rainier nodded up the slope to where Timothy Herd sat, holding a cigarette down by his boot while he looked through some binoculars, and bringing his hand up every time he smoked to cover the ember of the cigarette, as though this small glow in the broad expanse of night might make a difference.

"He's thorough," Ed quipped.

"All of us should be. Be careful out there, and if you're not sure, retreat. I'd rather a man to fight another day than another victim to bury."

"Yes, sir," Ed said while Captain Rainier turned toward Hank Lacoste, "Did you hear that, Locust?"

"Lacoste. And yeah, I heard. The important parts. Just point me where to set up and I'll go."

Captain Rainier looked off to the southwest and while he worked to pick a position for Hank Lacoste, Ed Broadstreet spurred his horse Marlin, and started at a canter away from the camp.

Nine

It was a bird that warned him. Embarrassingly, Segonkwa had not sensed the man's approach, and it took the motion of a sparrow darting from her nest in a thistle to alert Segonkwa to movement in what he had believed to be a dead and vacant night. Segonkwa was startled, but he was not so unprepared as to be unarmed, and the rifle, limp in his hands, snapped neatly to the crotch of his shoulder, and he sighted down the barrel, holding his breath to better hear the clop of horses' hooves on the nighttime pan. The horse's steps were quick across the stones, and the animal seemed careless of the gritty slides its passage caused. Segonkwa dropped to his belly and as he crawled forward through the spiny brush, reconciling himself that if there were more than two intruders, he would not have time to retreat to his horse, and a quick and bloody surprise was the best he could hope for.

A rider crested the rocky incline with his head bent to the ear of his horse, and Segonkwa was horrified that he had no shot to take, and that this first man already knew where he was positioned in the thicket.

The man was only a silhouette, a disturbance of the ebon void, an imperfection in the blanket of stars, as he broke the horizon atop the spine of the ridge. But, as quickly as he had arrived, he accelerated down the incline, and his silhouette was lost.

Segonkwa listened and the man rode his horse scrabbling,

chattering over the stony scree, but the pace was constant and unwavering, and Segonkwa lay, a silent witness to the passage of the rider on this night. Slowly his presence dissipated, the hoofbeats were lost, and their tick-tock sound rippled out across the plains until the night was once again dead and empty.

Segonkwa counted his breaths and watched the spine of the ridge with desperate intensity. He wondered if this man was not the main force, but a runaway leading a whole cavalry down on his head. He had seen no horses or prisoners in tow, but had also been so surprised that his memory formed a better picture of the man, filling in details, when he in fact had hardly seen a thing.

But no cavalry appeared, nor did any more birds disturb the air and signal to Segonkwa that he needed to be alert. But the moment would not leave him, and he tried to calm his breathing as he rose to his feet. Segonkwa meticulously placed his feet, every step measured and silent, travelling with no more sound than a shadow traverses the face of the moon.

Segonkwa returned to his hobbled horse, Fart, a name that came about because of a stupid bet, and a once-in-a-lifetime-shot by a big-mouth named Mackie. But when he was not in the company of the others, Segonkwa still called his horse Charles, his original name. He scratched Charles behind the ear then mounted and girded him with his heels to get him moving. Charles acquiesced and his powerful strides moved them quickly to the peak where the rider had passed, and Segonkwa rose up in his stirrups and surveyed the land, first for the rider, then to the south for any others.

He waited and the night protested that it had ever been disturbed, for the great dome of sky above was cloudless and seemingly fixed in a starry tableau.

Segonkwa left the ridge and rode quickly, arriving to a sober camp and a half-hearted card game that formed a semi-circle around an unlit fire. Segonkwa dismounted and didn't bother to hobble his horse, instead walking to Crooked's tent and rapping his knuckles on the tarp.

"Taylor, it's Gonk, I came across their other party."

"What?"

Surprise emanated from the men at the card game as well, and they tossed aside their hands all three of them. Hugo and Howard got to their feet, and massive Carlisle with a tourniquet around his calf just below the knee, stretched out his hands, and the other two helped haul his heft to his feet.

Crooked Taylor crawled out of his tent upon his hands, his crutches hanging by leather straps he wore looped around his shoulders in an 'X'. He rose to his feet by awkwardly scissoring his legs under himself, then balancing on the twisted limbs. He switched his hands to his crutches and lifted himself erect.

"What did you see, Gonk?" Crooked asked.

"One rider. He was moving at a pretty quick pace and wasn't careful of cresting ridges or leaving tracks. I waited and no one followed him, and I tried to find him again from atop a rise, but he's gone."

"Any uniform?"

"Military. Definitely military."

"How bogged down was he? Was he making an escape with stuff, or no?"

Segonkwa searched his memory as best he could, and outfitted the shadow of the rider he had seen with pack saddles and then without. "Not much gear. His horse did not have a lot on it."

"He can't be too far from their camp. I bet it's within two miles of where you found him," Crooked stated.

"We could make it in ten minutes," Carlisle offered. His face was shadow and what few teeth he had were like jagged chips of ivory outfitting his lopsided scowl.

"That calf plaguing you? You want a little payback, Lisle?"

"Yessir, I want a lot of payback. I think we all do."

"Well listen, much as I'd love to go, I'm not a man to disturb a card game. You boys sit down, finish up, we'll mount up after you're done." Crooked smiled and laughed and batted away his joke mirthfully, the men grinning along with him. "Gonk, go and gather Horntooth and Weitz from watch, tell them to come on back to camp and give their weapons a once-over."

Ten

Ed paused a moment to regard his listeners before he continued his story; "I was on night watch. I was placed to the north of camp and they came upon us from the south. I heard it start about a mile and a half, maybe even two miles back. Captain Rainier wanted his scouts placed far from camp to make sure he got plenty of advance warning if we saw something. Problem was, it took me so long to ride in and they were so many and so vicious, I stopped about a quarter mile out and popped off a couple of shots, but it was lost. I made myself enough of a nuisance that one came after me and I turned and rode like hell because I knew there was nothing I could do to save the men — they were mostly dead by the time I got there. Dead or rounded up. The one chasing me was on my trail for half the night, but at one point he crested a ridge at a fortunate time, and I shot his horse — injured it just bad enough that he fell behind and couldn't chase me any more."

Ed sighed and nodded at the flames of the campfire, and no one spoke as they regarded the little orange devils, tap-dancing amidst the dry chaff they fed the fire. Moses waited for what he believed was a respectful amount of time before launching his first inquiry. "How'd you get injured?" Ed looked up from the fire, and Jasper turned toward Moses still smoking; his pipe had become a constant chimney at the side of his head ever since camp had been settled, and it was as though the internal cogs and gears of the Father's mind were coal-powered and giving off great gouts of smoke as they worked overtime to think.

"When I rode into camp in the beginning I was on top of a hill," Ed explained. "It was a good vantage point, but they could see me, easy as I could see them. They launched a couple arrows my way, I caught one in the shoulder." Ed worked his arm out of his shirt and pulled out his shoulder, pointing to a small, puckered scar.

"Did the arrow even stick?" Moses asked.

"No, but it clipped something," Ed retorted. "Bled like a stuck pig and my shirt was red down to the wrist by morning."

"Did he have a lot of Indians with him?" Clarita asked. "Crooked I mean?"

"Some," Ed said. "Always had some with him. He was always friendly to the tribes; and I guess when the braves didn't feel like they liked the tribal life they were free to join him."

"He recruited people too," Calafort added.

"Yeah, I heard that," Ed agreed. "In Mexico he would hire Mexicans, in the territory, Indians, McCleod always talked about how smart Crooked was with things like that. It was one of his advantages."

"You talked to McCleod?" Moses asked.

"No, but the men that did passed it down and we all knew that Crooked would pay anyone he thought might be useful, color be damned. He even had a woman that rode with him for a while. Least that's what I heard."

"A woman in camp with all those sinners?" Clarita sniffed. "I'd rather be dead."

"From what I heard she could hold her own," Ed said. "Mark, up in the mountains, any girls with Crooked when they ambushed you?"

Unable to sleep, Mark had returned to sit at the fire, but he was sullen at his evening's thievery being thwarted and felt especially bitter to have had to send his handsome horse back to Aspirations, along with its opulent trappings. He had stolen all of the money from the saddlebags, along with a small derringer that already felt at home in his boot. But if Lougheed reported his things missing, Calafort had been stone sober, and may make the connection. Mark pondered how he might explain his possession of Lougheed's belongings and did not welcome Ed's disruption. "No. No women. Just criminals."

"He just collects all the scum of society and organizes it and sets it against us," Clarita said. "He's like a plague. I pray that the Lord has already seen to justice and that we don't find him alive."

"The Lord already sent our best man," Moses chimed in, "and he's ready to be fitted for a casket."

"Hey!" Ed snarled. "Have some respect! That man's the reason we're all here! And I'm sure McCleod didn't leave him in no better shape; there won't be much left for us to do."

"He didn't save you," Moses retaliated. "You wasn't there for the siege, you just come on in when it's safe and talk about riding in like a goddam hero!"

Calafort was silent but he clapped Moses a thunderous backhand across his cheek that caused Moses' head to nearly corkscrew clear off of his shoulders. One moment Moses was sitting, and the next he was holding his face, lying prone in the dust. Clarita opened her mouth, and her gaze was hard, but Calafort's black fury was overpowering, and she closed her jaw without a sound.

"You crossed the line, Moses," Calafort whispered. Moses turned onto his side and Calafort sat and gazed, smoke curling in rings about his bushy countenance. "We have all been through a lot, the Lord has tried us greatly, but I will not tolerate blasphemy. I am lenient but I have my limits; do not break the fourth commandment again."

"The fourth commandment?" asked Moses, bewildered.

"The Lord's name in vain," Calafort informed. The priest sucked on his pipe and Moses remained on his belly while the rest of the fire sat, like marionettes fastened by their cords into paralysis. Calafort acted as though he did not notice. He never ceased smoking and seemed content to sit and watch the fire.

Moses carefully picked himself up from the ground and returned to his seat, his eyes never leaving Calafort, as though at any moment another attack might strike. The sun had long set, and the moon was large and bright enough to cast its own shadows in the night. A coyote yapped somewhere on the plains and Moses held his face with one hand; the swelling made his beard feel bloated on one side and his mouth downturned and crooked.

They sat in uncomfortable silence until Father Calafort rose from the fire. He rose with neither word nor sound, and strode away into the darkness. Those still at the fire pretended to think until they heard him making water and then, after what seemed like a very long interval of silence, Ed ventured a question.

"Mark, were you in Aspirations? During the siege?"

Mark nodded.

"We were there," Clarita offered but Moses shook his head.

"Best let Father Calafort tell it, he saw it all. Probably best he do it, it's his story."

Ed nodded but when Father Calafort returned to the fire conversation did not resume. They sat for some time, and Mark was the next to leave the fire, saying his goodnights again as he headed for his bedroll, and a second attempt at sleep. With Mark gone the others soon retired, and one-by-one the fire's members departed, leaving Calafort as the last person awake. This large and lonesome figure sat and watched the fire burn down until it extinguished of its own accord, leaving nothing but the light of the moon upon the plains.

Eleven

"Coffee's up and bacon is cooking!" Calafort boomed, his voice like predawn thunder upon the prairie. "The day is alive with sunlight, and I can feel a soft breeze stirring!" Calafort transitioned into an energetic hymn, and he snapped his fingers in between prodding with his knife, the thick strips of bacon that sizzled in the cast-iron skillet. "I am a vehicle of the Lord, a vehicle to do his bidding! God's hand and mine, they act as one, evil of this earth ridding!"

Sleeping nearest the cookfire Mark was rudely awakened, and he nearly drew his pistol from beneath his pillow he was so out of sorts, until the powerful hymn of Jasper Calafort registered in his mind. He was doubly angry for having slept in because his original plan (hatched in the moments before fatigue snatched him into a dreamless sleep) involved his leaving prior to dawn. This plan could have helped in a number of ways, the first of which he might be able to get rid of the more identifiable items wrangled from Lougheed's kit, so as to make sure his own broken commandment was not found out by Jasper Calafort. Secondly, riding with Calafort and company permitted Mark no opportunity to rob.

Birds answered the harangue of Calafort's song, and camps a mile away were awakened by his singing. The verses rarely matched, and theme and story were absent, but Calafort's voice thundered enthusiasm and vigor, and seemingly brought all the world to life with its volume. Then, as suddenly as it had started,

Calafort's powerful hymn was abandoned, and he poured himself a mug of coffee and sat watching his camp, smiling at the late risers as Mark, Ed, Moses, and Clarita worked to dress and join him for breakfast.

For all that he had lacked as a man, one piece of good advice handed down to Ed Broadstreet by his father, was that the best cure for suspicion was confidence. While Ed could not remember the event that prompted this sentiment from his father, he utilized the brilliance of it now, and urged his pony toward Father Calafort's, riding side-by-side with the priest, leaving the other three to follow behind.

"Hey, Father, how far is it to where we're going?"

Calafort looked at Ed and smiled for his company, then turned his attention back to riding and beamed at the white sizzle of the heat on the flat pan they rode. "I heard a joke once," Father Calafort began.

"Sure," Ed invited.

"The man's name was Terry Stephaneau, a Frenchman, from France not Louisiana," Calafort explained. "After only a week visiting Aspirations, he said that he figured if the devil ever had a chilly day in hell, he could send people up here and they wouldn't notice the difference. I appreciate the joke regarding the heat but disagree that any part of Texas is hell."

"I guess it depends what you're doing in Texas." Ed immediately wondered if he had crossed the line, but Calafort showed no signs of his previous wrath, and laughed in agreement.

"That's true. I can see if someone was left off somewhere without supplies and had to walk any distance, they might think it hell. Although, I would amend that statement and say, as close to hell as this mortal form can achieve."

"That's fair, we can't know the real thing."

"No, we cannot."

"They said I should ask you about the siege. Moses and his wife I mean."

"Clarita. And, I don't suppose I have any special claim to the story, although I did live through it, yes."

"They just said I should talk to you and from what you're saying and what I'm seeing, we've got plenty of flat miles to cover until sundown."

"You make too many good points for me to disagree. However, I think an interesting chapter of the story actually starts with Moses."

"Should I drop on back then?"

"It's fine." Calafort waved away the idea and as the horses trotted across the chalky flats, he began to describe the siege of Aspirations Texas.

Twelve

It took Ed over a month to reach Cincinnati, and in that time this particular corner of the west boiled over. The massacre of Ed Broadstreet's abandoned party turned out to be the beginning of the campaign that led to Aspirations' entrapment, and as he made his way north, the horror of what he had done settled more deeply into his soul. The only word the military ever received regarding the murder of Ed Broadstreet's companions was what Ed Broadstreet delivered to them himself. However, this lone testimony was still superior to the news acquired regarding the second column; after receiving their orders from Major Lionel McCleod, no man from that company was ever seen again. With two columns wiped out, only the squad led by McCleod was yet to be accounted for.

By this point in time, Crooked Bradley Taylor had taken up and traded with enough Comanche that a good number of his band were composed of them. And, since the attacks were located deep in Comanche territory, the doom of the first and second squads was assumed to be by ambush from Indians who knew where best to do it. Crooked also had no problems trading with horse thieves, and even he himself had partaken in a midnight horse-raid once. So, compared to the ragged nags owned by the military, Crooked likely had the advantage of fresher, faster horses for his crew, and free passage across Comancheria to his heart's content.

The casualties estimated for both sides varied wildly

depending on the telling, but all were in agreement that when Crooked Taylor reached the Granite River his squad was haggard, desperate, and had equal bullets in their guns as their bodies. But their leader was fanatical in pursuit, and since Major McCleod was largely responsible for the military's crusade against him, Crooked's yearning for blood seemed focused entirely on McCleod.

Thirteen

Even as his uniform rotted away from his body, Lionel McCleod was religious about his hygiene, among other rituals. He awoke before dawn and left camp to check on the horses, then used his binoculars to spy on Hugh Gunn and make sure that the man was dutifully attending watch atop the ridge. McCleod did not lower the binoculars until he saw Hugh scratch himself. He made sure to see the man move, remembering when a scout of his had been nailed to a tree and made to look as though he were alive and on-duty. That mistake had cost McCleod a number of lives. Having confirmed that Hugh was on-watch, McCleod went to the river where he bent and drank the cold water, then wet his face before he pulled out a straight razor and artfully danced the blade back and forth across his sharp cheeks and chin, until his face was smooth like marble.

He chose to shave at a small ingress in the shore where the water pooled and was calm; far from the insidious undercurrents of the river that had almost drowned Benny Cunningham the day before. Benny and his horse had disappeared from atop the surface without a word and remained below-water until the frightened horse kicked its way free, dragging its tangled rider to the surface alongside it in a shrieking white froth. The men ashore threw out more ropes into the river than Benny had hands to catch, but he and the terrified nag were pulled ashore, and the whole troupe of them, made to cross at another location, further up the river from where they had camped.

When McCleod returned to camp Logan Freeroy was spurning the fire to life, the gray morning clouds dissipating as the sun grew brighter.

"Major," Logan said. He nodded his head and McCleod nodded in turn and was thankful that Logan was not a talking man; McCleod sat beside him on a stump and rolled and smoked a cigarette, while Logan prepared coffee in silence.

McCleod did not pressure the men to wake, as many of the horses still refused to stand from their hard ride the day previous. Breakfast would be a dry, cold affair, as it had been for the past two weeks. McCleod finished his cigarette with dissatisfaction and immediately began to roll another one, using his pantleg to rest the paper. His pants' seams were weary and splitting, and the color appeared permanently altered, as though desert sand had worked itself into the cotton fibers, staining them so deeply that they could never be navy-blue again. Despite his wretchedness, McCleod's kit was still in the best shape of any of the men in his service. Robin Cutler no longer had a rifle as the barrel had burst in his hands from misfire, and pistol rounds were limited in general.

From atop the ridge Hugh Gunn hollered, and both Logan Freeroy and McCleod leapt to their feet, McCleod spilling tobacco as he pulled his pistol free of its holster.

"Major! Major!" Hugh's words were muffled by the distance, but his whistles were piercing enough that the whole camp soon came awake, the men arming themselves as they all watched Hugh's buckskin pick her way down the slope.

McCleod didn't wait for Hugh to reach camp, and instead he mounted his horse and rode to the base of the ridge, aiming his rifle up toward the ridgeline in case Gunn was being pursued.

"They're not that close but they're coming!" Hugh shouted.

Spills of gravel slithered down the dry slope, and clods of grass churned as Hugh's horse fought to descend under control. He reached the bottom of the slope where McCleod was waiting for him, rifle across his lap.

"I expect we have a little time," Hugh told McCleod as he and the horse stood in the day's early light, panting from their descent.

"How long?"

"Fifteen, twenty minutes maybe."

McCleod received this information in silence, then turned his horse and spurred it back toward camp, Hugh Gunn kicking the ribs of his tired mount and beckoning for her to follow.

Fourteen

McCleod sat his horse halfway up the rough pine slope, but when Crooked Taylor and his company were within eyesight he descended and gave his horse to Alex Monaghan who led it away from the river and into the safety of a small copse of trees. McCleod joined his men at the edge of the river where they awaited their foe.

Crooked covered the final half-mile of ground with a white shirt tied to the nose of a rifle he held aloft and waved above his head while riding.

McCleod watched his men and tried to gauge their temperament toward Crooked's antics, and soon decided that it was best for him to speak.

"Nobody shoot unless I order you to do so. That is a direct order and I expect it to be followed." His comment was met with silence, so McCleod let the men return to their agitated state of silent waiting.

Crooked's own forces came to a stop a good distance from the river, so that when Crooked Taylor approached the water's edge with his white shirt held high, he was alone and a very tempting shot.

"Good morning, Lionel! I'm glad we caught up to you during the daylight — now we can speak in a civilized manner!"

Across the width of the river, the gurgle of the active current made Crooked's voice difficult to hear, but McCleod ground his teeth just the same, and stepped forward from his cluster of soldiers to confer with the bandit. He stepped carefully, and his right hand hovered near his hip while he walked, which Crooked seemed to find amusing. The white shirt atop the rifle quivered as Crooked laughed, and his mirth reverberated up the rifle butt that was resting in his lap.

"You planning to hip-shoot me from across the river, Leo?" Crooked shook the white flag at his foe as though in jest and nudged his mount closer to the river's edge. Major Lionel McCleod approached the river as well, and upon seeing this Crooked nudged his horse forward into the water until the horse was wet to the belly and Crooked's boots almost skimmed the churning surface. Crooked's horse dipped its head to drink, and he let the reins sit loosely in his grip as he held the rifle, and McCleod stood on the brown mud across the river, surveilling him.

"You can address me as Major McCleod." McCleod did not raise his voice to shout like Crooked, but his voice crossed the distance just the same; like a hard plank extended across the river.

"With our history? I'm not me without you and you're not you without me!" Crooked laughed and the force of the laughter was audible to McCleod from across the river. However, Crooked's taunting served only to reinforce McCleod's stony silence rather than to break it. "I know stories all get their own versions, depending on the teller," Crooked called out. "But, Lionel, there's nothing I'd love more than to hear the story you tell about how we first met. Or perhaps you don't tell people that?"

"What do you want?" McCleod demanded.

"You. Only you. Only ever you."

McCleod shook his head. "If you're not going to be serious, I'm through talking."

"I am serious!" Crooked asserted. "If you come across this river your men are free to go. This will all be over. Surrender yourself, McCleod. You and only you, and everyone else can go free. Nobody will harm them."

"I'm not falling for your tricks, Taylor!"

"No tricks!" Crooked shouted. The volume of his voice was rising, its pitch becoming more aggressive, and the white flag served as warning as the tension of his anger radiated up the shaft of the rifle and made it quiver like a dowsing rod. "It's never been a trick! Just none of your men live long enough to hear me demand it twice! Hand yourself over, I don't want anything to do with the others!"

"How can you assure us of anything you promise?"

"I can't but it's your only shot!" Crooked nudged his horse along the bank, travelling parallel to the river's course, and he turned his gaze toward McCleod's squadron of soldiers and addressed the cluster of men standing behind the major. "Your horses are probably about spent, I'm betting food is tight, and so far, you've still had ammunition when we've met, but that won't always be the case!"

"I could say all the same things about your men as well. From my count, I have six to five." McCleod countered.

"Sure. But Star of the Morning seemed pretty interested in the bounty I put on you, and she's not the only one I told. However, she's the one I expect you'll most have to worry about between here and Aspirations though — if I'm right and that's where you're going!"

McCleod could not help turning around to witness the impact that Crooked's words had on his men. They seemed unshaken, but McCleod had learned that with many men, external signs of the soul's disintegration tend to be one of the final signs. McCleod quit the bank where he had been standing and strode back toward his men, and Crooked seemed desperate to follow, riding his horse further into the river, his knuckles white as he gripped the reins tightly and forced his mount to stand in the current of the river up to its throat.

"Can you all hear him?" McCleod asked his soldiers as he joined the group.

"Enough," Milton Brent replied.

"He's tried this before. I lost a captain," McCleod explained. "The captain thought he was sacrificing himself for his men, but Crooked just killed him, then tracked down the rest of the men and killed them in a couple of days. If you all want to hand me over that's fine, I'll swim the river and leave you an extra horse, but my opinion is that six men is better than five, and there's no guarantee he won't just come after you like he did the other men last time."

Robin Cutler nodded while he held onto Milt's shoulder and stood on one leg, stretching first one thigh then the other. "How far to Aspirations, Major?"

"A hundred miles. Maybe less."

"I think you're right; we'd do best to stay together. Harder to kill six men than five."

"It flattens out to the east," McCleod advised. "A mile or so from the river the hills fall away, and you can see for quite a distance. How I see it, with six of us, we ride the flattest parts of the prairie so that we'll see anyone coming from a long way off. That way, we'll be able to decide whether to run or to stand and fight, depending on what we see. At least it will give us time to make a decision though." Finding no objections to what he said, McCleod permitted a rare smile to grace his hard mouth, just briefly, before he turned around to address the crippled bandit where he sat horseback in the river.

"Leo, tell your men I have a deal for them!"

"They can hear you just fine!" McCleod called, without leaving the group.

"Good because here's my deal! Me and my boys will ride west, as far west as you can see, and I'll leave only one man behind at the river here. He'll sit on that hill and stay on our side of the river," Crooked shouted, pointing with the bore of the rifle toward said hill, white shirt flopping, "and when he sees Leo cross, he'll come get him and escort him back to us. If I'm lying, what does it matter? You all will have a head start, and only one man close enough to do anything about it! What do you five say? Don't let him answer for you now!"

"We don't cut deals with outlaws!" McCall returned.

"That's what you say, Leo. Lemme hear another voice say it. Call across the river, one of you, call across the river and tell me why you five men want to die for your officer!"

"He's stalling," McCleod told the group. "He's up to something with all of this."

Crooked Taylor sat his horse and stared across the river, and when the group of soldiers began to move away, he picked up his rifle from across his thighs, jammed its butt into his shoulder and fired. The shot erred and a scud of dirt skipped on the river bank and McCleod along with every one of his soldiers, scattered like deer when the explosion severed the morning quiet. Each man took five or six steps in a separate direction, then cast themselves down on the ground and began a vigorous counter-fire.

Crooked's second round caught Milton Brent in the abdomen, his third shot missed, and he had no opportunity for a fourth, as he had to abandon his mount and drop into the river. Since Crooked Taylor was the lone target on offer, multiple bullets hammered into the side of his horse as he toppled from the saddle, and the animal spun and screamed in agony and fear and landed in a flailing pink-and-white-froth in the shallows. Crooked splashed into the cold running water and lost his rifle as he surfaced, thrashing his arms and dragging himself, dead legs trailing behind, crawling along his belly through the river mud and into the cover of the weeds.

By the time Crooked raised his head the majority of the salvo was over. He looked up and saw McCleod's men well back from the river, and his own companions rushing forward, but taking shots only hesitantly, as McCleod's soldiers disappeared into the trees, rejoining the horses that had been hidden a safe distance from danger.

Crooked waited to ensure that no soldiers came back, but the wait was unnecessary as no soldiers reappeared. He crawled out of the weeds on his hands, in the direction of his horse, but Segonkwa was already beside the animal and speaking calmly to it as it snapped its teeth and lashed the air with its hooves.

Crooked drew his pistol and pulled the trigger but it misfired, and without a word Segonkwa unholstered his, handed it over, and Crooked shot the horse in the eye. The shot rang out singular and clear, and the animal's mad frolicking ceased immediately, the body moving only in small twitches.

"Damn shirt was heavy, threw my aim off," Crooked complained.

"You wouldn't have hit him anyways," Hugo said as he joined Crooked and Segonkwa on the riverbank.

"Probably true, but the shirt is a good excuse, right?" Crooked laughed and propped himself up on his elbows and looked over the motionless beast beside him. "Dang. I really liked this horse."

"Not enough to name it," Segonkwa pointed out.

"Names are hard to remember, and numbers seem cruel, so that just leaves me without naming them."

"You're lucky Brindle bit it, you can have his horse."

"We're not lucky to lose Brindle. You're never lucky to lose a man like him." Crooked's voice adopted an immediate and unexpectedly cold tone, to which both Hugo and Segonkwa were taken aback. "He was awful at poker and thought he was great. There's nothing better than a fool who's proud to give away his money." Crooked's face lightened and he laughed then said to Segonkwa, "Grab my crutches, I think they're tied on the other side of the saddle."

"They're here," Segonkwa said, bending down to untie the implements.

Crooked lay on his belly, filthy with river mud and soaked from the water, but judging from the mad spirit alive in his smile, one would think the encounter with McCleod had gone well.

Fifteen

Crooked sat atop Brindle's wiry bay, the creature all tendon and bone. Frustration was harbored in the cores of his green eyes and made the pupil seem lively with fire. He surveyed the land, and the sun was bright but big cumulus cloudbanks jockeyed for position across the firmament, blotting out the sun from time to time. The ridge on which McCleod had positioned his scout stretched for half a mile before it dropped into a valley, the other side of which a luscious golden stretch of prairie grass was being gently combed, all in the same direction by the wind.

"I don't think they're running," Crooked said, his voice amplified by the silence of the landscape about. Segonkwa, Hugo, Carlisle, and Howard Orr sat their horses, none much heftier than the stringy mare beneath Crooked Taylor.

"Give it time," Hugo advised. "They'd be stupid to burn daylight sitting around here."

"Unless they know something we don't," Crooked said.

"Do you mean about the river?" Segonkwa asked. "But this is where people cross." It was written in the trees scarred by hatchets and the campfires, and the naked patch of ground skinned of grass, and filthy with left-behind rubbish.

No sooner had Segonkwa expressed this, than six horses began to ascend the hill toward the golden prairie grass, two miles distant or so. It attracted the attention of all five outlaws, and they watched the speed of the horses and, not one for excessive bouts of silence, Crooked was the first to speak. "Look at how played out those ponies are, and McCleod and his boys giving us a show; he has 'em all riding nice and tall and staying in formation." Taylor snorted laughter. "I know I shot one of 'em right in the stomach, no matter how tall he's riding right now, he'll be cursing me later if he isn't already."

"Think they'll dump him?" Howard asked.

"McCleod's a coward," Crooked spat. "It's his weakness. He's a coward, and he likes to hear people call him brave. He'll leave 'em behind if he needs to, but I think he's gonna try and stick with them all the way to Aspirations." Crooked turned and swatted his horse on the rear, as he could not dig his heels into its ribs, and Brindle's horse responded with a side-step, not moving closer to the river.

"Forward dammit! You're not much better than riding a chicken as it is, if you're afraid of water I'm putting you down and walking," Crooked cursed. He followed his comment with a second, harder slap to the mare's backside, and she shimmied sideways, then reared up onto her hind legs unexpectedly. Crooked fell out of the saddle and was left clinging to his horse's neck while she kicked the air with her wet hooves, his crutches tangled in their straps, and dangling about his shoulders. Horse and rider toppled into the reeds near the shoreline, and without legs to brace him, Crooked was dunked underwater. But Crooked rose, spluttering and growling, and with the reins still in his hands he slackened all tension from the leather, then pulled with great violence, wrenching the horse muzzle-first onto its side with a splash. Crooked flung himself upon the creature as its hooves gashed the air and kicked at the brown water and green reeds, trying to right itself. Taylor fought through the legs and grabbed the horse by its hackamore and roared at the animal "Is this what you're afraid of?" Crooked proceeded to shove the horse's head underwater but the animal twisted with fright and tried to stand, pulling Taylor off-balance and throwing him into the river once more. Taylor flung himself upon the beast as though never tasting defeat, and he belted the animal's head with punches then re-looped his hands in its reins and dragged it head-first into the water, using the weight of his body to submerge himself and the horse both. The horse wriggled free and emerged from the water, while Crooked sat in the shallows, panting, as his nemesis regained her feet. "This isn't an excuse to be tired later. This drowning was your fault, for not following directions, you hear?"

The horse stood in the shallows and snorted mist from her nostrils and Crooked collected his waterlogged self and crawled up into the saddle once more. "All right, forward. You got that? Forward." Taylor slapped his horse's rump repeatedly, and this time, the animal waded out from the shore and the tide of the river crawled up her flanks until she could no longer reach the bottom with her feet, and she was forced to swim.

Segonkwa and Hugo followed without their horses putting up any fight, but when Crooked was about twenty yards from shore he and his horse disappeared from the surface of the river.

"Where's Taylor?" Hugo asked.

"He was there?" Segonkwa said, unsure of what to think.

Both riders held their rifles overhead in one hand, sparing them from the river, and using their second hand to hold the reins of their horse.

"I think Crooked went under!" Carlisle called from onshore.

No sooner did Carlisle make this remark than Crooked resurfaced, spluttering, and shouting for the men to turn back.

"Turn around! Don't cross! Turn around!"

While Crooked shouted this his horse shattered the surface into a white froth like a porpoise breaching, while Hugo and

Segonkwa both felt the pull of the river's malevolent undercurrents.

Crooked shouted for the men to turn around but the horses felt the undercurrent too, and they began to panic, thrashing their heads from side to side and shrieking.

"Bail off, Hugo! Don't get kicked under by your horse!" Segonkwa called as he abandoned his rifle and mount both, diving into the river.

Carlisle and Howard could do nothing but shout useless directions from shore and watch the struggles of their comrades, while the horses they sat pawed the ground and groaned with sympathetic fright, for the struggles of their fellow horses.

Sixteen

It was well past noon by the time the horses were gathered. Crooked's use of Brindle's horse would be no further than their ride into the river, because somewhere along its struggles the creature fractured a hoof, so Crooked gladly put it down. However, the crew had no need of riding double because Hugo's body had been found, snagged on a deadhead floating in the shallows, two miles downriver from the crossing.

Crooked himself had descended into the water, abandoning his crutches and half-falling half-plunging from the bank to Hugo's side. He hugged the lifeless body to himself, and wriggled up the bank, never releasing Hugo from his embrace, and it took the interruption of Big Lisle, hauling the tandem up and beaching them like a pair of flaccid fish, to terminate the unsuccessful rescue.

Crooked lurched to his feet, balancing on his scissored legs, and Segonkwa handed him his crutches, though Crooked could neither respond, nor take his eyes from the face of his dead compatriot. "A river," Crooked said. "Hugo. No last name. R for runaway branded on his cheek. Killed by a — by a damn river." Crooked's voice betrayed his devastation, and it cracked with emotion.

"How'd they get across? That's what I'd like to know?" Segonkwa mused.

"They probably didn't. They probably had a better goddam scout than we do, one that would know when a river was too goddam swollen to cross." Crooked whirled on Segonkwa, his eyes aflame. "You should've looked closer," Crooked reasserted. His face quivered and he redoubled his effort to sneer, then abandoned it and began to laugh.

"What am I doing? Boy would my daddy be ashamed of me."

"Your daddy?"

"Yessir. Daddy would've told me 'Don't cry for a slave!'" Crooked's laugh seemed forced and he slapped his wet pant leg with a thwap and shook his head, but his mirth collapsed to a decrepit finish, and he snarled instead. "But I guess if my daddy were to say that I'd have to shoot him." Crooked spat, his face twitching with the palsy of his anger. "I dunno what McCleod is worth in terms of money, but if the universe were to balance him against Hugo on equal terms, the scale would break in Hugo's favor, ten times over and with change to spare."

Crooked took off his hat and flapped the sodden wreck, then shook his shaggy, unkempt hair, and replaced his hat and spat on the ground again. "Let's get this grave dug so we can get back to hunting, shall we?"

The rains responsible for the river's size and current had also made the soil moist. Hugo was wrapped in a strip of sheeting cut from his bedroll and laid into his grave before the signs of his vitality had even had time to recede. After the dirt was replaced from whence it was dug, the troupe stood to gaze upon their completed work.

"I guess we should say something," Howard mumbled. He patted himself for his flask, swatting himself harder with each successive pocket that he checked, as his desperation mounted. Eventually this perturbed Crooked and he said, "well are you gonna say something or keep slapping yourself? The hell's wrong with you, Howard?"

"Tryin' to find my damn flask," Howard said, his left hand still actively probing his body.

"It's in your right hand!"

This was true, and Howard looked at the flask, then shook it, and found its volume disappointing, owing to how liberally he had sipped from its contents while digging.

"Are you gonna speak up, mush for brains?" Crooked spat at Howard.

"Probably better you do it," Howard admitted, capping his flask after a healthy swallow.

"Damned if I don't do everything around here," Crooked said. He took a moment to compose himself, and Hugo's grave seemed to have a chilling, sobering effect.

"He was born a slave," Crooked pronounced. "That's all the world will see, but goddamit, he was a man I wouldn't replace with any other. I'd trade two or three of these slags to have him back again." Crooked tried to throw a grin over his shoulder, though Segonkwa noted that, despite Crooked's attempt, two moist trails traversed the bandit's cheeks, wetting the top of his beard. "Hugo looked at his life and demanded better. The world told him what he was worth, and he disagreed. Fought the world every step of the way, and I'd say he won more than he lost. He made a go of it. No back steps. No apologies. No excuses. He was tough, I'll never forget him, and he was a man that deserved better." Crooked turned to the men around him. "I'm not leaving anyone else like this," he told them. "We deserve better. We're not ending up in some back-country grave where the twig-cross is going to fall down in the first good wind."

After a long interval of silence Segonkwa recommended to the others that they go check on their horses, and Crooked remained, not for long, but just long enough to share some final words with his longest-tenured ally.

Seventeen

Every hour they rode and failed to see riders on the horizon, served to increase Crooked Taylor's anger. Rest breaks became less frequent, and when the bandit dismounted, he lurched about on his crutches, berating the men and animals with a ceaseless torrent of jokes — some of which were barbed enough to let the men know to hurry.

But the troupe was eventually forced to stop and make camp, when the shadows melded into the oncoming night, such that they could no longer be sure of where they were steering their horses. A sea of grass lay in their wake, yet Crooked turned and squinted angrily at his presumed lack of progress.

"They can't be in any good shape," Crooked declared. His crutches were wedged in his armpits, propping him on his feet while he used his hands to hold a dented tin cup of coffee, and a cigarette simultaneously. In between gouts of smoke and sips of coffee he gazed with displeasure at the flat prairie around them. "We should've seen them by now."

The men knew better than to speak to Crooked when he was angry, and Crooked's rage had been building the whole day through. Perhaps the calming presence of Hugo could have been a balm to soothe this flame, but without him, Crooked spun himself into an angry whirlwind of threats, some muttered, some said jokingly, and some eliciting a twitch in the corner of his mouth, from whatever dark thoughts he was thinking. He smoked and drank his coffee quickly, as though wanting to hustle through a chore.

"Lisle—" Crooked cut himself short, rethinking his question, then out of nowhere he began to chortle. "Hah! Never mind. Stupidest question of my life. Segonkwa, how tired is your horse? And, Howard, how's yours?"

"Tired," Segonkwa said.

"Mine's about done-in," Howard agreed.

"Well Hugo's mount is a better bundle of glue than he is a horse, and that's when he's well-rested." Crooked said no more, instead setting himself upon the task of sipping and smoking until he pitched the nub of wet paper into the darkness beyond where the campfire could light. He readied his horse which balked at being re-saddled so soon, but Crooked was in a vicious temper and he rapped the horse on the nose with the butt of his pistol and it cowered until the girth strap was cinched and did not complain when the bandit climbed up his side, hoisting himself into the saddle with the strength of his arms.

"There's no way they're far," Crooked seethed. "I'm going to find them."

"And do what?" Segonkwa asked.

Crooked shrugged and smiled, and with his sun-reddened face further blushed by his unhinged temper, his smile was evil. "I don't know. Just be a pest, see if I can stir up some trouble for McCleod."

Lisle sighed and took a large swig of coffee before dumping the rest into the dirt beside him. He rose without a word and Howard wavered by the fire, still processing Lisle's actions through his drunken haze.

"You're going to kill the horses with this pace," Segonkwa said. "And it's a long walk to anywhere that we're welcome."

"I'm just going to kill this horse," Crooked promised. "For the rest of them I have a plan."

Eighteen

They had ridden hard and rested little, and Milton Brent had to be strapped into his saddle after he fell unconscious from blood loss. When they stopped for the night Milt was awake, but his lips were blue and his brow no longer sweating despite the heat. The men unstrapped him and eased him down from the saddle, laying him in the naked grass, as no one had yet had time to unpack their own effects. McCleod had not even dismounted and instead stood in the stirrups of his saddle and fought the mounting darkness through the spyglass he had brought, searching the western horizon for pursuers. The sun was set and only its pink aftereffects colored the clouds, but, short of discernible movement, the prairie seemed all the color of blood and frozen in this amber half-light.

McCleod dismounted and placed his hands at his lower back, extending backward, before approaching Milt and kneeling down beside him. He picked up his hand and whispered for Milt to squeeze, and the pressure he got in response was feeble like a newborn's grasp.

"How long's he got?" someone asked.

"Minutes," McCleod replied, keeping his eyes on Milton while he held his hand.

"Could we give him any water?"

"It'll just leak out."

Milton's shirt looked black as though it was soaked in oil, and the bloodstain plunged down his leg and into his boot like an indigo ink spill.

"You men rest. I'll tend to him. If he has any last words I'll take them down," McCleod said. His words sounded enough like an order that the soldiers broke apart and began to make camp. This despondent little gathering, huddled below the cathedral of heaven's vault, had been settled for no more than an hour when gunshots began.

Every man sprang up, and a general commotion broke out as they collected their weapons, all of which were within arm's reach.

"Steady, men! It's me! It's McCleod! I am returning from scouting." McCleod knew the danger of riding into a startled camp in the dark, but the light from the stars was generous, and the men's dispositions were not so frightened as to be unresponsive to orders. "There are no shots coming at us. The shooting is some miles off yet."

McCleod's stern tone settled the fraying nerves of the soldiers, and as their eyes adjusted to the light provided by a brilliant spread of stars, they saw the gunfire lighting the darkness a great deal away, with many miles of featureless prairie in between.

"We might be in luck," McCleod declared. "It looks like Crooked Taylor ran into a little bit of trouble chasing us."

This observation fit smiles onto the faces of the men, but they did not lay down again until the gunshots had ceased, and no more started up for a period of five minutes. Guns were loaded, every one of them within their grasp.

Nineteen

The devil gave no rest to McCleod and his men that night. Not even an hour elapsed since McCleod's hasty return, and another volley of gunfire ruptured the great silence, previously blanketing the land. In the wake of the gunfire, the scout Hugh Gunn rode back into camp similar to McCleod had done, and with great déjà vu the major had to shout for the men not to fire upon their own member.

McCleod mounted his horse and glassed the gunfire with his telescopic eyeglass, and from his observations, the gunfire seemed to originate from a single source.

"Everyone lay back down; it's not but one shooter, and they're quite a piece off yet. Much too far to do anything more than make noise."

The men lay down, but the gunfire remained a regular occurrence all through the darkest hours of the night. Its proximity neared with each successive series of explosions, and all of the men remained awake, despite being under orders to rest.

The evening lands were not quiet for more than fifteen minutes, when the quiet was intruded upon once more, by the thunder of gunshots.

"Major—"

"Quiet," Major McCleod demanded before the speaker could say more. He mounted his horse once more, the poor hobbled creature serving for observation deck, half of the hours it should have spent resting, and while peering into his spyglass,

Major McCleod stated, "the shooter isn't going to reach us tonight; he's travelling slow, likely he's riding a horse too played out to even run. I will keep watch. All of you rest."

The men did not sleep, because whether an inch or a mile was being covered between intervals, the shooter announced himself regularly, like a perverse cuckoo clock, accelerating the time between alarms, such that the fusillades were sounding every ten minutes. Many times, McCleod debated ordering the men up and riding out, but that was what Crooked wanted. Instead, McCleod's iron will kept his soldiers pinned to the ground, peeking their heads up like gophers, but still horizontal as per his command.

However, Crooked Taylor did not stop sounding his rage from out of the darkness, and eventually, Major McCleod ordered the men up; well before the sun even hinted at an arrival. The east was night sky and hard desert, welded together black on black, distinguishable only by their difference in texture. The men shoveled food mechanically into themselves, trying not to flinch as they swallowed cold hunks of salted beef, gunshots echoing in the background. They suffered breakfast without a fire, and water was all that was consumed to drink before the men were mounted, and on the move once more.

Twenty

It was not hard for Segonkwa and Howard to locate Crooked Taylor. They needed only to point their failing horses toward the most recent series of gunshots. They did not see Crooked until they were quite close, and he caught their attention by standing up from where he was seated, on what turned out to be the ribcage of his dead horse.

"You got any ammunition left?" Segonkwa asked as he and Howard rode their sweating horses up to Crooked's position.

"Always," Crooked said around a cigarette he tucked between his lips. He leaned his armpits against his crutches as was his habit, and fished in his breast pocket, locating a match to strike, and set fire to his cigarette.

Howard and Segonkwa pulled up their reins, but there was little need as the horses' gaits were little more than a crawl.

"So, what's the plan for today?" Segonkwa asked. He and Howard dismounted, and they began to release gear from the horses when Crooked stopped them.

"Don't strip those horses. We're going soon as Segonkwa's ready to ride again."

"We doubling?" Segonkwa asked Crooked.

"Not unless I'm wounded. No, Howard is going to stay here, guard Hugo's pony, you and me are going to give McCleod and his bunch a good chase."

"How? There's no way we can catch them," Segonkwa said. "Crooked, look at them, the horses are string and bone."

"We don't need to catch them," Crooked said. "We just need to ride at them hard, put some fear into them. I'd rather Aspirations be full of a bunch of scared men telling stories, than men riding in and talking like they won."

"But what do I do here?" Howard asked.

"Drink. Nap. Lisle's gone to see Star of the Morning, see if we can't convince her to redirect her crew toward Aspirations with us," Crooked said.

"So, I just stay here, cook in the sun and get drunk?" Howard asked.

"Like I said, Lisle will be along, and he'll be bringing horses and people aplenty." Crooked said to Howard, before turning his attention to Segonkwa. "When you're ready to ride, ride that horse until it's done. Shoot plenty, just like I did, keep them scared. If you can try and drive at them from a flank, make them think you might overtake them from one side or another, that would be great."

"What about you?" asked Segonkwa.

"I'll try and cover as much ground as I can with this one but still keep him fresh—"

"It's a her," Howard interceded. He had taken his assignment quite seriously, and his flask was uncapped, and he had no intention of screwing it on again.

"Keep *her* fresh, and push to catch up with them if I can."

"Crooked, they're too far ahead—"

"Don't start lecturing me." Crooked's mood clouded immediately, and he spat out his half-finished cigarette and let it smolder in the dirt. No one spoke and Crooked crutched over, and despite his own previous command, began to strip Segonkwa's horse of its saddle.

One bag of water, and his crutches were all the gear that

Crooked brought, in addition to the small arsenal strapped around his waist. Crooked slithered up the unsaddled horse with his gear slung around his shoulders, then arranged his crutches behind him as he took the reins in his hands.

"Strip that other saddle and hand me those reins." Crooked glowered back and forth, splitting his ire between both of his comrades. "Change of plans; I'm taking both of the horses. You two wait for Lisle, I expect he'll be along in a couple of days."

"Crooked—"

"Make your way east toward Aspirations. I'll meet you somewhere in the middle."

Segonkwa wished he could alter Crooked's course of action, but ever since he had first met the man, Bradley Taylor had been hellbent on this current course of action. Bradley's anger was a runaway train, and Segonkwa did not know how many bodies would lay on the rails before the train was stopped, but he feared that the number would not be small. But Segonkwa reminded himself that Crooked Taylor could take all the hearts that the world had to offer and still not be satisfied, but if he were able to gaze into Major Lionel McCleod's eyes as he perished, then he would need no more violence until the end of his days. Or at least this is what Crooked Taylor professed.

Segonkwa did not speak as he unsaddled Howard's horse. Crooked received the reins with a sneer, and then the man beat the flanks of his bare-backed horse with the butt of his pistol until it accelerated to a pace that suited his urgency. Mineral dust from the horses hung in the air, little sparkles catching the early morning sun, and tracing a tail behind Crooked Taylor; a comet streaking on an unalterable course toward its own annihilation.

Twenty-One

Surprisingly, the first horse to fail was the one that Crooked towed, and so the beast was easily discarded by uncoiling the rope from around his waist, while both horses were still on the run. No sooner was the rear horse released, than its hoofbeats dropped away, and the panting wreck stood slouching in the crystallite dust raised by Crooked's last serviceable animal. He wrapped the horse on the rump with his pistol barrel, hard enough that its withers contracted in pain, causing the animal to stumble.

"Dirty mule, don't you dare," Crooked seethed, another in a countless string of profanity heaped upon the animal he rode. But the horse was done. It stumbled with any pace above a trot, and he battled its failing strength for every mile he now rode.

"Go! Go! You aren't done yet you bastard!" The horse applied an unexpected burst of speed, in response to a particularly vicious hammering from Crooked's pistol-butt, but this encouraged the horse to lope over a bush where it's feet became tangled, and it fell. Crooked was tossed from the horse and he skidded through the dust in his shirt sleeves, attached to the horse by one hand at the reins, his hat lost in the fall. Crooked rose to his feet simultaneous to the horse, and he gripped the reins in one hand and drew his pistol. He fought his way atop the mount and then shot the top half of the horse's ear off, causing the poor animal to scream and take off at a gallop.

But despite his instillment of terror, the horse's muscles could no longer fire in smooth, synchronous fashion. The wheezing carcass of horseflesh clattered along, a marionette whose strings had become entangled. Half-collapsing, the horse plodded, with legs quivering like a newborn's, before its back end dropped-out and it fell for a second time. Crooked made no attempt to rouse it.

The bandit bled from a cut above his eye, acquired in the first fall he and the horse had taken, and without his hat, the blood had hardened into a brown crust on his cheek under the afternoon sun.

"Try and survive, I'd love a ride back," Crooked said to his horse. The animal lay unresponsive but for the rise and fall of its ribcage, and Crooked patted himself, finding his crutches, water, and pistols all in order. He turned his face skyward where the sun hung like a peach, so ripe and so low, one could almost reach up and pluck it from the firmament forever; it would take but a gentle tug.

However, across the desperate miles that had culminated in the collapse of three horses, Crooked was awarded with a little rooster tail of particulate, shining in the east, to mark the passage of McCleod and his horsemen. It was the first he had seen of them since the river, and this newfound proximity seemed to reignite Crooked with a hatred that was inconsolable.

"McCleod!" Crooked howled. He could almost visualize the sweep of his voice, echoing across the breadth of the prairies, and the satisfaction caused him to chuckle before he launched his next volley. "McCleod!" Crooked shouted again. He paused and listened to the dissipation of his voice in the empty air, then pulled his left-hand pistol and fired three shots in quick succession.

Then Crooked began crutching as fast as he could. He swung and planted, swung and planted, reminiscent of a bird or an amphibian; an animal designed for another task, but now stranded upon the earth, and forced to locomote as best as his disadvantages might allow. But catching his objective mattered not, because Crooked could see with his keen eye, the broken line of horizon caused by five riders atop six horses.

"Wonder where they left that gut-shot fella... Wonder how I could have missed seeing him." Crooked spoke to himself as breath raked back and forth through his teeth, the sweat stains beneath his arms expanding as he crutched across the desert.

Crooked looked up and his adversaries were still atop the distant ridgeline, and so he bellowed, a concussion of anger leaping up from the base of his chest. "McCleod...! McCleod!" Three more gunshots barked in the wake of his howl, then Crooked stuffed his empty left-hand pistol back into its holster and did not bother to reload.

He leapt into motion once more, setting aside the throttling headache attacking his temples, and the blisters caused by the crutches chafing his armpits, and the accumulated miles of riding, working to bury him, while he stood in such close proximity to his destiny; his encounter with Lionel McCleod.

Twenty-Two

"He ain't got no more horse."

"Must've rode it to exhaustion."

"Then what the hell's he still doing?"

McCleod could no longer ignore the constant backward glances of his men, and their childlike trading of fears back and forth.

He turned and glassed the evening prairie, finding one lone form, struggling stubbornly forward, despite the vastness of the world around him.

"He's a cripple with too much energy. Nothing worth gawking at," McCleod stated. He turned his telescopic lens in the opposite direction of their pursuer, toward Aspirations.

The town was not yet visible, but McCleod spied the eastern slope of Stone Hen ridge; grazing land owned by Moses Louis-May, who swore that the early-morning light meant better grazing for his cattle. All the grass looked brittle as hay to McCleod's eye, but he supposed early-morning dew might fortify it from the wasted state he was looking at.

Regardless, Aspirations was within sight and their adversary was now without a horse. Alone and lurching through the twilight, Crooked looked like some deranged and half-broken machine that would not die, imbibed with the terrible life of his devil's heart.

"Private Cunningham—"

Two gunshots, and then the bandit's voice, calling across the emptiness, a cry composed of only one name.

"McCleod...! McCleod!"

"Major?"

"What?" McCleod asked.

"You started to say my name," Benny Cunningham said.

Major McCleod found himself mesmerized by Crooked's approach, forgetting what he had started to say.

"McCleod!" Crooked cried, stopping just long enough to fire two more shots.

"Let's go," Major McCleod said, his voice a throttled whisper. "Let's head to Aspirations."

McCleod turned and spurred his horse and did not look back, fighting the near-physical pain it caused him. The men had a choice either to sit where they did, or to follow the man that had brought them back to Aspirations, when in all likelihood none of their other comrades could have done so. The men behind McCleod turned their horses, although none of them appeared to be in a hurry to ride away. It was left up to the horses to guide themselves, because even once they got their mounts moving, the men were too busy looking back at the slow advance of the bandit, to worry much about where they were going.

Twenty-Three

"Hold on," Mark demanded.

Although Father Calafort had directed his narrative toward Ed as the two of them rode side-by-side, the day was without a breeze, painfully hot, and the silent griddle of the salty flats seemed to amplify sound.

As such, Father Calafort found Mark interrupting his narrative, while riding almost twenty yards behind him and Ed.

"I'm supposed to believe," Mark began, "that five full grown men, and one of them Major Lionel McCleod to boot, turned tail and rode away from a cripple hobbling through the desert? Five men in rifle-range against a cripple with no horse, nothing but six-shooter pistols, and none of them thought to stand and fight? After all we lived through in the siege, and these ninnies — Major McCleod excluded of course — but these ninnies couldn't find the gumption to try a shot or two?"

Mark spurred his reluctant horse to make up the difference between him and Calafort and Ed, and he joined them, riding now three abreast, as he continued to insert his opinion. "Seems like a golden opportunity they wasted; could've just opened fire and been done with." Mark said.

"I just remembered, you're not from around here, are you, Mark?" Now Clarita inserted herself into the conversation, and the conversation was paused as she rode up to join the men, Moses grumbling at her side. "Clare, I don't care what the cost is, I'm using salt on this canker-sore inside my lip — it's as big as a toad wart!"

"What's that, Moses?" Ed called, not quite hearing the man above the clop of the hoofbeats, all five horses now riding abreast.

"It's nothing, and no you're not, hush, Moses," Clarita snapped.

Moses made a sour look and pulled the brim of his hat low over his eyes to show that he was no longer paying attention.

"Anyways, Mark, I was remembering that you aren't from around here," Clarita repeated.

"No, ma'am," Mark said. "I ranged across the territories quite a bit, Texas only some, but north as far as the Yellowstone River — further even."

"And what about south?" Clarita inquired.

"That's where I was born."

"Whereabouts?"

"Nowhere abouts. My parents were travelling when I was born, I came to them on the road one night and they weren't sure where they were exactly, but they knew it was Mexico and my mother always hated that."

"Hmph," Clarita said.

Twenty-Four

He could not ask his son to plough, for Bradley could not keep pace with the harrow, even towed by the slowest oxen. Most sons could till a row, help their father in some way, and if his mother had not been barren (save for the twisted wreck she managed to spit out) Ernest might have had some properly formed sons to do man's work.

It was true, that when loaded carefully with a yoke, Bradley could crutch a great load of weight, and his grip became like smithed steel because he hauled water up from the well with only his hands, he shoveled snow and hay; though never pretty, the boy was competent enough to accomplish most any manual task one could do while stationary.

Ernest resented the maldevelopment of his only child, and so he began to court whores in town in the hopes of getting one of them pregnant. One night while drunk, he pondered aloud whether Hannah his wife, had vindictively fed him something, so that he was no longer virile enough to reproduce. The walls were thin, the fight was loud, and Bradley heard it all.

Ernest blamed the failing of his farm on his cripple son and barren wife, but greed drove Ernest toward a quick solution, and Bradley learned a good deal about carpentry as he and his father renovated the bunkhouse such that it could be rented out to guests. Little Rock had no shortage of visitors, enough for the small bunkhouse turned residence to have two to four sleepers on any given night, and every week or two, someone requesting a nicer room, would pay double to bunk up at the main house.

Bradley Taylor was charming in all of his interactions with guests. They tipped him generously, and some of the longer-tenanted patrons even taught him about instruments. Bradley's father never paid him for his work, and so Bradley grew proficient with his music. He never passed up the opportunity to toss a hat on the floor and produce a harmonica from his pocket, or to sit down at the keys of the dusty piano in the lounge and conjure up pleasant melodies from the oft-forgotten sarcophagus. Bradley made sure that his father never saw the tips, although one time a close encounter forced Bradley to swat his hat under a table so quickly that the majority of his tips were scattered, left to the dishonest fingers of patrons leaning down from their stools.

The pretty young girl did not shout her request for a song, but instead waited respectfully in the courtyard as the oak tree's leaves chattered overhead, brittle in the autumn wind. When Bradley stopped his nimble fingers from dancing upon the strings of his fiddle, the pretty girl asked him, "do you sing?"

"No, ma'am," Bradley answered. "The purpose of my music is to attract customers, not to send them running."

She laughed. Her hair was delicate and red like the feathers of a phoenix, and her eyes so blue that they could fill the prairie sky with envy.

"Let me see your smile," she said.

Bradley tried on a sheepish grin, but the girl tsked with disapproval. "That won't do. I'm afraid you'll go poor if I don't lend you a hand."

The girl touched Bradley's arm, steadying herself as she set her bag on the ground, then she smoothed the wrinkles in her skirts.

"What songs do you know?" she inquired.

"Hold on, how do I know you're a good singer?" Bradley asked.

"How do I know that you know how to play that?" The girl returned, nodding toward Bradley's fiddle.

"Didn't you just hear me playing it?"

"I heard you trying to strangle it."

Bradley laughed and so did the girl, and he said to her, "may I at least ask the name of my musical companion?"

"Matilda. And yourself?"

"Bradley."

"Charmed to meet you, Bradley. Now, let's choose a song." The afternoon grew cool as the sun dipped below where it could light the courtyard's dust, but the onlookers appreciated the melodious duet, emanating from the crippled boy, and the girl who was so pretty she was painful to look at.

Bradley showed up to the courtyard the following day but did not see Matilda. Two more days of waiting in the gusty courtyard as autumn stripped the oak tree of its leaves, and he gave up looking.

Bradley did not see hair as beautiful as Matilda's, until when at the age of sixteen, he rode into town with his pocket full of tips from busking. Bradley wore both of his pistols strapped high about his slim waist, and he lowered himself down from his horse, while a crowd of men smoked and talked in the shadows cast by the lee of Morris Hall. Bradley unstrapped his crutches from behind his saddle, then looped his horse's reins around his wrist, and crutched over to the hitching post to tie his animal off.

Bradley was nervous, and he paid more attention to the men outside Morris Hall than to his task, but the group continued to laugh and shout, and they showed no signs of caring about anything other than their drinks. He hitched his horse without issue, then patted the pistols at his hips, before crutching through the batwing doors that led into the dilapidated, two-storey building whose roof bowed toward the floor and was decorated with multi-colored pieces of lumber, depending upon the age and state of weather-corrosion, experienced by the specific repair. The windows held no glass, outfitted by flimsy shutters alone.

Upon entering the cloistered confines of the barroom, someone called out to Bradley, "Hey! Hey, boy! What whiskey you drinking?" Bradley turned, but before he could speak the cross-eyed drunk guffawed and turned back to the group, huddled around the low table. "I want what he's drinking! So darn potent, now his dern legs won't work!" The men hooted laughter but it seemed directed at the speaker, so Bradley crutched past them, into the enveloping smoke.

Buck Newsome finished the whiskey purchased on his behalf, a donation from someone drunk enough to take pity on the scrapheap of a man. His clothes looked like discarded rags piled upon a dirty, hump-backed ox, and he drank the whiskey quickly and angrily, tossing its fire into the back of his throat. Buck saw Cherry ascending the stairs and leading the crippled boy toward the second level of Morris Hall. Buck had traded his pistol, plus a lucky hand that won him some coins in blackjack, all to purchase a romp with Cherry the night before. Drunk and sullen, Buck could not abide the twist-leg abomination taking her upstairs when he himself did not have enough money to get proper drunk. Neither Bradley nor anyone else in the barroom expected his behavior, but Buck rose from his seat and walked across the uneven floor of Morris Hall before he snatched the whippet of a boy from the stairs by the scruff of his neck and pitched him to the floor. Buck's meaty fists found a gentle, juvenile face to smash, which Buck continued until he was wrestled away by a scrum of men cursing his stupidity.

"Stop it! Damned fool!"

"Buck, you dummy, you know who's kid he is?"

"His daddy's gonna send a whole squadron of marshals down on us because of you!" A mob of men wrestled Buck away from Bradley, the boy bleeding and stupefied from the unexpected attack.

Buck shrugged himself free of the men blanketing him, like a moose ridding its hide of blackflies, but Bradley cursed him from the floor, his words sounding slurred as he tried to talk past three loose teeth, a split lip in need of stitches, and a mouthful of blood. "My father has nothing to do with this," Bradley called. "But you're not going to beat me blindsided like a dog again." Bradley crawled over to where his crutches had landed, collecting one then the other, and rose to his feet and clicked toward Buck, glowering up at him, as though there weren't a head of height and a person and a half difference in weight between them. "Are you willing to fight me like a man, or do you always win by jumping someone from behind?"

"I'll squash you like a bug you broken-legged mutt. Someone shoulda put you down a long time ago."

"Looks like the job has fallen to you," Bradley sneered.

Buck did not own a pistol, but Hobbie Hanmer lent him one, briefly explaining that its barrel pitched left, and the hammer stuck somewhat and needed a strong thumb to be pulled down. However, Bradley's words whipped Buck into a wrathful frenzy, and he practically foamed at the mouth as the two of them abandoned the shadows of Morris Hall to do battle out in the heat of the afternoon.

The distance was thirty paces. Bradley Taylor looked like some awful sacrifice propped upon his sticks. The boy was barely thicker around than the crutches holding him up by his armpits, and this tripod-like posture leaning on the crutches, made Bradley an exceptionally stationary target. Opposite stood Buck Newsome, mountainous, and seemingly half-gorilla, due to his stooped posture and sloping hunchback. Buck claimed to have spent his boyhood stooped in the back of a skinning wagon, and it was this profession that produced both his enormous strength and his hump; considering Buck's seeming inability to smell himself, his claim to a boyhood spent skinning seemed quite plausible.

"Hey, hunchback, are you able to count to three? Or can we just draw like men?"

Buck drew. He may not have owned his own pistol, but his thick hand moved faster than expected, and it drew the pistol and got his shot off in one clean, practiced motion. The shot stayed true too, and would have ended Buck's little opponent, had Bradley remained standing in place.

Instead, as Bradley drew his own pistol, having predicted that Buck would draw when insulted, he let the crutch from his draw-arm drop away, and so Bradley fell to that side, and flopped out of the way of the shot. Bradley shot second but he took more time with his aim, so his bullet found his target, just below Buck's collarbone.

Buck was so large his torso barely registered the impact, a shiver and a grunt comprised his reaction, as a red blossom began to spread its petals across his chest. Wounded, and watching his first shot miss, Buck became frantic and shot off two more rounds wildly. Neither shot was well-aimed and so the dirt behind

Bradley, and five yards left, coughed up plumes of dust, until the third shot jammed the antique pistol in Buck's grip. Buck shook the pistol angrily, but he felt as though a great weight had been placed upon his breast, and the effort it took to breathe forced the large man to stumble and then sit down.

Bradley Taylor lay on his side, his own pistol trained dead center to Buck's chest, but Buck's pistol misfiring offered Crooked the opportunity to rise, and he did so without hurrying. He rose to his feet as though deaf to the bovine wheezing thirty yards away, and Bradley took care to dust his shirt and set his hat properly upon his head.

Bradley clicked across the scuffed dirt yard separating himself from Buck. The crowd had hallooed with excitement during the duel's brief flash of violence, but now, regardless of their state of inebriation, every man and whore present was rapt and silent in observing the exchange.

Bradley stopped in front of Buck, and Buck was snorting, bloody strings from both nostrils and a fine pink mist flecked his lips as his fingers attempted to eject the spent pistol shells from their cylinder. Bradley used a crutch to swat the pistol away from Buck, and it tumbled out of his reach with a puff of dust, fine as chalk.

"Too bad it jammed," Bradley said. Buck's bleeding had progressed to the point that his lips had begun to pale, but he leaned toward Bradley, feebly reaching for his nearest crutch. Bradley hopped back and out of the way without issue, but Buck's effort landed him on his belly, and the quick exertion cost him many pained breaths and mouthfuls of blood. "I meant too bad for you," Bradley said. "If you kept shooting, I would have had no choice but to kill you. But this is better."

The boy's face was ruinous. His lips were asymmetrical, and his chin slathered in blood. However, the men of Morris Hall moved aside as Bradley approached the door on his crutches. It was quiet enough that his clicking steps could be heard, roaming the barroom until he found Cherry and asked if she still had his money.

"Course, it's right here," she said, offering forth the bills he gave her before the attack from Buck. "You want it back?"

"Nope. I need some company now more than ever. C'mon."

He nodded toward the stairs and Cherry, wide-eyed, led him up to the second level, turning around every few steps as though to make sure he was still behind her.

Cherry's room faced out toward the front entryway, but Bradley requested they move to a room in the back. When they arrived, he crutched straight to the window and threw open the rotten shutters, looking down into the yard where Buck still lay, untouched and unaided.

Twenty-Five

"I figure it's something he practiced a great deal," Calafort finished. "His dueling technique." Calafort wondered what effect his story might have on the morale of the hunting party, but his original hesitancy in releasing all of the details was overcome by the knowledge that this same man might still remain as more than just a story in the world. Until the body of the man was witnessed, cold and without its animating hate, fear of Crooked Taylor should not be set aside and retired. "He's been clipped in a duel before," Calafort offered. "It was one of his legs though."

"I'm guessing he goes both ways just as good," Mark inserted.

"Hmm?" Calafort asked.

"His leaning, falling trick, he can fall either left or right in a duel?"

"Yes, from what I know that is correct," Calafort affirmed.

Mark laughed, "I guess if he was always falling to the same side, someone would've figured it out by now."

"Probably," Calafort agreed.

"He might have a preference though," Mark suggested. "Like, if Crooked knew that the man he was dueling was a good shot, maybe he would use the hand he prefers?"

"Sure, but nobody knows which hand he prefers," Ed said.

Mark blew out his lips in frustration. "Well, then someone should've just done the right thing and shot him in the back, or while he was sleeping."

Twenty-Six

The day was tired from its exertions and so the sun swooned in the west on its way to a pink sunset. The horses nickered to one another in the stalls, and the dirt in the corral was churned fresh and brown. Paxton sat atop the corral's fence chewing an unlit cigarette and waiting for Grady to finish shaking himself as he pissed behind the barn. The call for dinner had been hollered and its echoes were dead, and Paxton was not known to be patient with his appetite. "Grady, did you not go all afternoon? Good Lord, man, I've heard horses empty themselves in half the time."

"Go on up to the house then, you know the way," Grady called over his shoulder.

"Mary-Anne gives me grief every time I show up without you, she thinks it's impolite."

"Well stop jawing at me then if your grief is with Mary-Anne."

Paxton paid Grady no further heed. On the crest of the hill to the west, the silhouette of a rider appeared, a dark shadow impressed upon the sun-swept clouds. Paxton was about to ask Grady if Thurmond (their fellow ranch hand) had been sent to Aspirations, but the rider appeared to be half the size of Thurmond and was approaching from the wrong direction.

Grady walked around the barn hitching up his jeans and Paxton hopped down from the fence and chewed the cigarette between his teeth with nervousness.

"I swear, you sit around while there's work to be done

ordering folks around—"

"Grady, shut up."

Grady looked at Paxton's face, then followed his gaze and the same leaden weight settled in the pit of his stomach. All of Aspirations was abuzz from the two lost companies of soldiers. There was nobody with ears who hadn't already heard three different versions of the tale, and the hyper-alertness of Aspirations' citizens caused the two young cowboys to nearly choke on their fear.

Paxton looked toward the barn and visualized the Winchester hung high on the wall above the tacking, then glanced toward the ridge where, to his dismay, the rider had increased the pace of his horse, with a second mounted horseman following in his wake. Neither rider's garb was worth description, ruddy brown as the land around them, but wrinkles, etched by the sun into the dark leather of their complexions, denoted both men as far from young, and of Indian descent. They wore braids of hair so black it swallowed the light, their fantastic coils like intertwined filaments of midnight.

Paxton started to walk toward the barn in what he hoped was a casual-looking manner to the approaching riders. But his plan was foiled before he had taken his third step when the lead rider called out, "Please move away from the barn." Paxton froze, for the voice of the man was a hissing serpent on the wind, and he called out a second time, forcing his smoker's croak to reach them. "Please, just stay there."

The horses trotted to a stop and the two Indians looked down at the boys. Opposite the two men on horseback, the boys turned to children, and the tomahawks and knives and pelts and details of these wasteland surfs petrified their souls.

"How many are you here? On this ranch?" the second,

smaller Indian asked, his voice regular, and harboring no rasping croaks. Paxton looked at Grady and Grady Paxton, then they turned back to the speaker, baby owls with bulbous eyes. "I want you both to answer at the same time, and the numbers better be the same," the second man warned. He held up three fingers and then counted down, "Three. Two. One."

"Nine!" they both said, although Paxton choked a bit as he spoke.

"How many women and children?" the speaker asked. Paxton and Grady both wore such unadulterated looks of terror that the speaker spoke in a gentler tone as though to assuage their fears. "We're not here for a fight. We're not going to hurt anyone, and we don't want your horses. We're here to tell you to stay away from Aspirations. "CROOKED" Bradley Taylor sent us to inform—"

A rifle cracked and the speaker pitched backward off his horse in a loose tangle of limbs. He fell into a surprised heap, and his first reaction was to reach for his pistol. The Indian with the smoker's croak whirled his horse about and slid down over the side of his mount, clinging to it side-saddle, in an attempt to take cover behind the animal's torso. Three rounds snapped in quick succession, causing welters of blood to erupt from the flank of the mounted-man's horse, while the man on the ground began to fire his pistol at the boys.

Nearest the barn, Paxton reached cover uninjured, but Grady was shot in the calf and then when he stumbled, he was shot through the neck before he could stand back up again. The second round barely registered to Grady, and he resumed crawling through the dirt, his injured leg strung out behind him while his neck bled freely from both sides.

Paxton ran out from the cover of the barn to grab Grady, and he dragged him back to safety in a stooping crouch, trying to stay low as bullets enlivened the evening-time air.

Grady looked down at the wound in his calf, but Paxton clapped his hands on either side of Grady's neck wound, and felt the warmth of his friend's pulse, as each heartbeat surged out through his fingers. "Pax, what happened?" Grady asked.

"Shh, just stay down!" Paxton said.

But the fight was finished. Moses Louis-May came running from where he had been hiding behind a tuft of chaparral, on the far side of the corral. Both Indians were shrinking in size as they galloped back in the direction they had come from, the smaller of the two doubled over in his saddle from his wound. The evening returned to its former silence, populated by the trilling of insects, the faint cry of desert birds, and the quiet wheezing emanating from Grady. Paxton held his hands to either side of Grady's neck until Moses knelt down and pulled his hands away.

"He's gone, Pax."

Paxton withdrew his hands reluctantly, and Grady sat propped against the wall of the barn, his eyes open, looking wildly surprised by all that had just taken place.

Twenty-Seven

"There's drafts in my blanket...I think there's holes in this ratty old thing, why would we choose this for travel...? I can't get warm."

"Charlotte, can you help Gramma get comfortable?" Connie would have tended to her aged mother herself, but she was occupied in trying to keep their mule-drawn wagon on a straight course, due to the undependable exertions of the family's mules. Thunder was old and moved steadily and mechanically forward. He was nearly impossible to get moving, but once he did, his momentum could seemingly carry him forever. Conversely, Beans ran in fits and spurts and was as hard to control as a housefly. Thunder kicked at him from time-to-time when the reins between them tugged to his disliking, adding to the bumpiness of the wagon's travels, and the difficulties of the pilot trying to keep the whole commotion in order.

"Mama, Joachim keeps grabbing the book!" Charlotte called.

"Read out loud," Joachim pleaded.

"It's bumpy and hard to see, I can't."

"I'm cold, pull the tarp back."

"Leave the tarp where it is," Connie snapped. "It took me an hour to fasten it down. Joachim, help mother fix her blankets so she's comfortable. Charlotte, read out loud so both you and Joachim can enjoy the book."

"But he keeps grabbing it and it's bumpy!"

"I want to see if there are pictures!"

"There are no pictures!"

"You haven't read it before; you can't be sure."

"It's not a picture book."

"Unfasten the tarp so I can get in the sun, I'm freezing."

"Mother, leave the tarp alone! Joachim, leave the book alone!"

As the occupants of the wagon bandied back and forth the wagon jostled irregularly, until their hubbub was silenced by a call from without.

"Hold it! Stop!"

Connie turned to face the road and the curious young faces of Charlotte and Joachim protruded from the canvas flap of the wagon bed, staring at the men spread out across the road, while Gramma fiddled unsuccessfully with one of the ties holding down the wagon's tarp.

They came to a stop where five horsemen stood facing them, blocking the road with their stationary mounts. None of the men dismounted, though the one nearest the wagon explained their intentions.

"Ma'am," said Big Lisle, taking his hat off of his head as he spoke. "You're going to have to turn around and head back to Aspirations."

"What? Why? I can't! We can't!" Connie burst. "I have my mother and daughter and son with me, and my mother is sick—"

Lisle waved his hand and Connie stopped her disorganized explanation. "I'm not asking."

"Listen, sir, please," it took only Lisle shaking his head for her to stop. Her eyes were magnified by tears, and the two children had retreated such that only their eyes were visible now, peeping out from a crack in the slit canvas.

"Turn around, ma'am."

"I don't have much money, but you can have anything you want," Connie attempted. "Anything we don't absolutely need to get to Monroe you can have for yourself."

Lisle shook his head and spurred his massive brown bay to the side of the wagon, towering above Connie as he spoke down from the height of his horse. "I don't believe it's right to draw arms on a woman, but I will. Turn your wagon around and go back to Aspirations and tell anyone you see coming this way to do the same."

All five of the men wore looks that informed Connie that there would be no negotiating.

Lisle watched her closely as she began the arduous task of turning the wagon.

"Are we turning around? Why are we turning around? Connie, why are we turning around?"

"Mother, hush!"

Connie tugged the reins of her mules, when a nearby explosion of guns caused her to pitch down the reins, and dive into the back of the wagon. She landed on Charlotte and Joachim, holding them close while draping herself over the top of them. Thunder and Beans took flight, each in a different direction, and the wagon leaned and hitched and bucked with their mad attempts at escape.

The episode with the wagon was not yet complete by the time the shooting ceased. Smallwood slid his colt dragoon back into its saddle scabbard, and the absence of Lisle's skull from above his eyebrows, marked the most severe of his injuries. Lisle fell and gray matter tumbled from the vault of his skull, while nearly a dozen other wounds wet the sand around where he crumpled from his horse.

"I think that headshot's mine!" Smallwood shouted. He dismounted, Howard followed, and then so did the two Indians. The quartet took their time hobbling their horses, and the Indians spoke their own language until Smallwood cussed at them.

"Hey, keep it American huh? Say what you mean to say for all to hear."

One Indian smiled, so small and willowy he looked like a jockey standing beside his gray horse. "Don't be scared. Makijkid Nahoe." The second Indian laughed.

"That ain't American," Smallwood seethed. He walked to his horse and fetched his dragoon then walked back to the two Indians, his tantrum seeming to have no effect on either of them. "Wanna bet it'll misfire?" Smallwood pointed the dragoon at the small Indian, prompting him to laugh even harder.

"Killing me kills you slowly," the small Indian said.

"I don't like riddles," Smallwood returned.

"Kill me, Ahotnao kills you. Kill us both, Black Rattle will cut off your hands and peel the skin from the soles of your feet, then lead you behind his oxcart until you fall. Black Rattle does not untie a man from his oxcart until his jeans wear out, and they are the last part of a man to come free in the sand. Sometimes he drags skeletons for weeks, waiting for the jeans to surrender. They say he needs no water to cross the desert because vultures revere him so highly, the old ones will lay down and die for him to eat, so that Black Rattle can live to fetch them more bodies. How do you think he came to possess the name? When you travel by night and your cart is noisy, people will call you such things."

Smallwood had no response, although the rusty gears of his

cognition could be seen attempting to conjure up some threat of his own to meet the one he was faced with. But the small Indian turned his attention to Howard.

"Howard, do you have any problems?"

"He wasn't the worst guy I knew," Howard said as he gazed toward Lisle's body. "But it had to be done. I mean, I did what I could, I didn't get no headshot like Smallwood, but I figure I emptied my whole pistol, so two or three of those holes came from my shots."

"Fine."

The small Indian turned toward Connie and the occupants of the half-turned wagon blocking the roadway. The small Indian walked toward the wagon and as he did so, he unlaced a leather thong from his belt and allowed a large round stone to drop, hanging from the string. Connie watched the man approach, and the rock went from hanging stationary, to spinning wildly, to embedded in the side of Mother's temple, all in the span of a single moment. Mother was still pale, and her brow furrowed, as though she were about to complain of being cold.

"Before we arrived," the small Indian called out, snatching Connie's face and clamping his hands over her mouth, before she had time to register a single scream. "Two bandits ambushed these poor folks, surprised them, and ran them off the road so that the poor old grandmother died in the crash." The small Indian leapt nimbly up into the back of the wagon, wrestling with Connie until he sat on top of her. "The terrible bandits had their way with this poor woman; each of them did," he shouted, slapping Connie's hands aside as he tore at her dress.

"Thankfully," the Indian pronounced, "the children were left alone, because even these bandits had manners."

Connie shoved the man away from her, but a fantastic volley

of punches began to rain down, forcing her to cover her face.

"We came upon the bandits by surprise, and poor Lisle did his best, but the bandits got a lucky shot off."

Connie whimpered as her clothing came free, and the Indian pronounced to his comrades, "Lisle will get a grave. But after we killed the bandits responsible for such terrible deeds, we dragged them off the road and left their bodies for the coyotes, so there won't be any point in looking for them."

Twenty-Eight

Aspirations was a small town even by frontier standards, and its happenings were usually no more interesting than the direction the wind was blowing. This had been the state of affairs ever since a young Captain McCleod had chased off every Comanche, Apache, Mexican, or other non-American he could sight in his crosshairs. And so, Aspirations now stood as a promontory of Christian light, jutting into the howling void of the godless wild. Long gone were its origins as a desolate survival ground; nowadays, doors went unlocked — for a wife had no need to fear leaving her door open late — for her drunk husband to wander back home.

In the central square of the town, the stairs leading up to the gallows' stage were gray from age, each and every board worn marble-smooth from an army of condemned boot heels that had trod over top of them. The gallows had its stanchion replaced, but McCleod ordered that the stairs never be removed; many of those to be hanged kept their eyes on their feet, not wanting to look upon the crowd, or the noose itself. McCleod snatched away this last vestige of sanctuary, and the walking dead could approach their doom with certainty that, regardless of their ultimate fate, legions of men had ascended those boards before them, and so wherever they ended up, they would not be alone.

The old men in the parlors of Aspirations had memory of a time when a pillow felt wrong without a pistol contouring it from beneath. They spoke of midnight vigils, huddled in the center of their houses with pistols cocked and a single candle set near the door to make sure that the shots would all be sent in the right direction.

The invaders had howled long into the night, yipping and herding horses up and down the avenue before disappearing into a creosote dawn, and the only rain to fall all that summer.

But that had been only once.

When Connie Lancaster stumbled into town, she arrived wearing very little of her dress, and holding the hands of her daughter and adopted son. But the children were more propping Connie upright than she was leading them, and soon a mob of people appeared in order to extract her story and gobble up the details. And also lend a hand. Connie was not grievously injured, but it took Father Jasper Calafort's force of person to extricate the poor woman from the hungry mob. He plucked her from the center of attention and sat her on a low adobe wall, then knelt in front of the poor woman, holding her hand gently and coaxing her toward a description.

"Take your time, Connie, just take your time telling us what happened," Calafort said. Connie's face was bruised, and her lip was puffy and bleeding. Between whimpers she attempted to inform Calafort of the travel ban, but her words were largely insensible. Instead, it was Joachim's explanation that furnished the crowd with the information they so desired.

"He made us turn around and said no one else could go on the road."

"Who?" Calafort's attention, along with the assembled onlookers, focused on Joachim like a searchlight, and Joachim wilted under such intense scrutiny.

"The man," Joachim mumbled.

"Was he on crutches?" Calafort asked.

"No. But he said he works for that man. The man on crutches."

Father Calafort visibly stiffened upon hearing Joachim. His face lost its sympathy and became the face of a man of boundless capacity. A man capable of anything. Capable even, of nailing a man's hands in a hug around a poplar's trunk then whipping him to death for what he had done to a little girl. Keaton had agreed with the punishment, but his guts had failed him in its application, and it had fallen upon the priest to both crucify and execute the man. And he had done so with that same hardened look, as though none but God himself might stop him from performing what was necessary.

It took all of Father Calafort's influence to pry apart the mob and scatter its occupants toward more useful tasks. He led Connie and her children into the cloister of the church where Calafort boiled coffee for Connie and offered the children some "coffee" as well, for handling themselves like such capable adults that afternoon. In reality, Charlotte and Joachim were given mostly warm milk, with a dribble of coffee for color, but they both swelled with pride when offered the same drink as the adults. But whatever serenity the town regained in the wake of Connie's entry, evaporated as soon as the rampaging squadron of Moses Louis-May and his ranch roared into town, shouting to every citizen with ears, that Crooked Taylor himself had just attacked their ranch, murdered one of their ranch hands, and the rest of them had barely made it out alive.

Twenty-Nine

Gossip arrived at Aspirations more quickly than citizens could rightly orient it in their heads, and as the final whispers of sunlight dissipated, Bug Calhoun rode into town at a clipping pace. The streets were silent, and Bug sat low in his saddle, weary from numerous miles in the sun. A citizen of Aspirations all his young life, Bug could not help but experience a flood of terror at the town's current appearance. Torches were lit and swung from baskets and wires cobbled together, as though the citizens of Aspirations were waging war against the night itself. The main street was alive with the orange light of fire, but the buildings beyond were dim, their windows black and vacant of life.

The face of each building held three or four torches, much more than was required to find one's way beneath night's starry cathedral, but if fear was marked by the admonishment of darkness, then Evan's Metals was the highest rung of heaven. Evan had set so many torch-holders into the front of his store, that when looking at his place of business Bug could locate no actual wood of the storefront before the offensiveness of such excessive lighting forced him to look away.

Evan's Metals, a wall of fire, and Bug turned his horse and trotted up another lonely lane, his eyes questing for some vestige of familiarity among terror-stricken abodes, alien to Bug, and a sorry blow upon his soul.

Thirty

Beneath the failing amber sky, Crooked Taylor sat alone in front of his tent. He had no fire, and his tin cup and spoon, along with his iron skillet from dinner, were scrubbed and sitting upside down on a flat rock to dry. The noise from Black Rattle's camp surged, the thin, tinny voice of Black Rattle distinguishable for sounding like shearing metal and accompanied often by his own laughter. As another volume of mirth receded, the sound of footsteps crunching upon dry stones could be heard nearby. Crooked did not move at all, save for his eyes darting to the top corner of their sockets.

Arthur Coe materialized from the sunset's murk, and the slender man coiled his legs and lowered himself to the ground in a cross-legged position, identical to Crooked except for the shape of their respective limbs.

"Don't look so glum. You'll still get McCleod," Coe told Crooked.

"That's all I'm here for," Crooked whispered.

"You had to have known right?" Crooked shook his head slightly but Arthur Coe did not accept this, and he leaned toward him, closer than was necessary to relay his words. "Somewhere, deep, deep down, try and look for it. I promise you it's there."

"Stop it," Crooked said.

"Oh, Bradley, you poor little babe. You can't hate that bad and expect to see clearly." Crooked's pistol was cocked and positioned against Coe's nose before he could move.

"The nice thing about you not having anyone left is that your threats get really dry really fast," Coe said. Crooked pushed the gun into Coe's face, dimpling Coe's cheek and forcing Coe to tilt his head backward to avoid the gun barrel's pressure. With his head cocked back Coe's Adam's apple ran up and down along the cord of his throat as he laughed. "You wanna talk about dry threats? That pistol of yours."

Coe swatted it aside and Crooked replaced it against his forehead, but this time Coe leaned into the gun and grabbed the pistol with both of his hands, cradling the revolver like a lover's face he was about to kiss. "I love the curvature of the cylinders; they remind me of a woman through the hips; the most beautiful contours."

"I doubt you say that in a second," Crooked growled.

Coe smiled and used his thumb to stroke the pistol between his hands affectionately. "Bradley, if you shoot me, you don't get McCleod. You know that. This little trigger of yours," Coe said, tickling the mechanism with the tip of his finger, "might as well be a hundred miles away for how much control you have to pull it." Crooked sneered and Coe released the gun and tenderly brushed at Crooked's cheek with a thumb. "Hold still, there's a little something here, maybe food."

Crooked used his other hand to slap Coe's hand away, and Coe leaned forward and planted a kiss on Crooked's lips. Crooked swung his pistol at Coe, but Coe rolled away and stood grinning, like a child excited by their mischief.

"And still no bullets! Not a single one!" Coe called in a singsong voice. Turning his back on Crooked, Arthur Coe pretended to be holding on to a partner and he waltzed about, spinning with meticulous steps, until he arrived upon Crooked's crutches. Coe ceased his imaginary dancing and picked up the crutches, bringing one of the implements right up to his mustache to scrutinize it, as though he was looking for something in particular.

Crooked holstered his pistol and pulled himself along the ground toward Coe, and Coe giggled and stepped away from him, keeping the distance between them equal.

"See, here's the problem," Coe said. He stepped away and Crooked pulled himself forward a second time, but the titter of laughter caused Crooked to stay put when Coe moved away from him again.

"C'mon. C'mon. You can do it. Just a little more effort!" Coe cooed at the man, stranded upon his belly.

Crooked took out his knife and spat with anger as he threw it uselessly toward Coe. Coe put one crutch beneath his knee and strained until it snapped, and repeated the process without urgency, allowing Crooked ample time to watch.

"You could have shot me, kept your crutches intact, and suffered nothing," Coe said. He threw the broken crutches in the direction of Crooked. "But look at you. You're weak. McCleod is your weakness and you let everyone know it. You became so focused on your own selfish prize that you stopped playing the game. And now you're angry because you lost? You are like a horse being led around by the reins, people can take hold of your motivation and steer you this way and that."

Coe turned and strode away, not toward Black Rattle's congregation, but toward his own tent and fire, set far apart from the rest of the men.

Thirty-One

The church was gossip and perspiration. Cigarette butts were trampled beneath nervous feet as citizens scurried about, elbowing, and apologizing and kicking and scratching and blaming others for their rudeness, while the mob surged like water in a shaken bucket; swirling back and forth in a roil but with nowhere else to go.

Bug almost lost his hat in one such wave and stumbled sideways. He saved the hat, but unfortunately his elbow caught little Elizabeth Turner on the bridge of the nose. It was left to Paul Turner, to cup the red faucet beneath his darling's face, and Bug jimmied his way between two arguing women to try and apologize for the accident.

"Hey, Paul! Paul! I'm so, so sorry!"

"Here, Lizzy, you grab onto Mr. Bug and stay with him while I look fer yer mother!" Paul transferred the weeping, bleeding girl to Bug and she clung to his sleeve, while Bug wondered whether it would be rude to fetch away his arm and roll up the sleeve to save his best shirt from getting stained. Ultimately Bug decided the blood was adequate penance for his mistake, although he simultaneously disagreed with his need to be punished; he had merely been tossed by the crowd's momentum.

The crowd was approaching its boiling point when McCleod and Calafort entered the room, bringing with them Moses and Clarita

Louis-May. Even among the nervous smoke and tumult of the church's main hall, the crowd was sensitive to these new additions, and silence quickly descended upon the congregation, without a single citizen needing to hiss for quiet.

Calafort looked at McCleod, but McCleod's eyes were already upon the crowd and his gaze was a pry bar that could not be bent.

Bug Calhoun remembered how perfectly visible Major McCleod was. He was neither on horseback, nor taller than average, but the immensity of his presence seemed to occupy more space than merely his corporeal being, perhaps this aura of power was tangible to some effect by the desperate crowd. Regardless, the crowd's volume was so stifled by the entrance of Major McCleod, Bug could hear Elizabeth gulping air through her mouth so as not to disturb the silence with her effusive nostrils.

"I'd like everyone's attention please," McCleod said, as though he did not yet possess it entirely. "It has been determined that right now the outlaw Bradley Taylor has taken control of Aspirations' roads. It is not safe for anyone to attempt to leave. Men of fighting age, please follow me. The rest of you remain here with Father Calafort. He will explain the rest."

For a military man the speech was coddling and long-winded, but the citizens of Aspirations were used to less flint in their public addresses.

"What's fighting age?" someone stammered.

McCleod's eyes spotted the speaker with ease, and Jed Campbell tried to shrink down into the surrounding congregation; Jed was obviously of fighting age but had levied the question regarding his twelve-year old son.

"Twelve," McCleod stated. His voice was cold and did not

waver one iota. He spoke quietly, and then exited, but his words loomed in the air, long after his physical departure.

"Twelve and up, follow Major McCleod," Calafort called, prompting the crowd to break apart and start moving.

Thirty-Two

McCleod had few words for the men who followed him out into the courtyard. As for words of encouragement he offered none, and his instructions were laconic, direct, and expected to be understood without repetition. The saving grace for many of the men was Calafort's knowledge of the talent of his flock. He sent a dozen capable women out into the courtyard, and McCleod repeated his orders with grave reluctance, which allowed some of the men a second pass at the information.

They were to arm themselves. Thoroughly. Firearms of all sorts were welcome and would not be persecuted regarding their age or condition. McCleod explained the value of a cache of loaded weapons; one could throw down an unloaded gun for a loaded one, continuing to fire, and thereby increasing the efficacy of each soldier.

Hand-to-hand combat was possible. McCleod warned against blunt knives, explaining that they would go in easily enough, but retrieving a rusted blade from an enemy torso was near equivalent to losing it. Hoes, rakes, scythes, poles, brooms, anything long and sturdy that might unhorse a man could come in handy.

Upon dismissal, the parcel of men and women selected to fight, left the courtyard like a pack of desert squirrels; they skittered between patches of cover, all eyes and limbs and fear, but smiling every one of them, as though this false application of confidence might help. But the fighters returned in a devil's procession, parading their scavenged modes of destruction in flickering orange pantomimes as they wandered about in the town's torchlit aura. Sporting an armada of mismatched blades, they were knights armored in coveralls, bearing rifles of indeterminate origin, quality, and length, some of which looked dangerous for the user to fire.

Cleveland Parker showed up asking for a gun, as he claimed to possess only a sack full of rocks. There were too few rifles already, but when the rocks made an unnatural clinking sound, Cleveland's sack was investigated, and it was discovered that Cleveland had raided Evan's metals after Evan left, stealing a sackful of doorknobs. A fight was avoided only by ordering Cleveland to return the doorknobs, and he was supplied with a spare claw hammer as a replacement weapon.

Thirty-Three

"This is ridiculous... This is ridiculous." If Otto Wagner's smoking correlated with his nervousness, then it was obvious for all the men to see that the intervals between emptying his pipe bowl of its ashes and refilling it anew, were steadily growing shorter. "He can't just barricade a town. For one man?" Otto turned to Robin Cutler, one of the invaluable remaining rangers of McCleod's. "McCleod ain't able to save us."

Cutler shrugged and looked at Lou and Jerry who were sitting beside one another on the room's small cot, both of them showing an abundance of faith in the integrity of the bed, as it bowed toward the floor, and its overstretched springs groaned with every minute shift. The men sat identically, leaned forward with their arms crossed and buttressing themselves on their knees. "Take a seat Otto. Your pacing ain't doing no good, but making us nervous," Jerry said.

"We should be nervous," Otto replied. "Hell, we should be terrified, every one of us!"

"I dunno that this is helping," Lou said, in agreement with Jerry.

"It won't help to keep our heads buried in the sand neither!" Otto said. "McCleod has got the Comanche all riled up, a tribe he ain't even fought before, and he's brought them down on our heads, in addition with the most wanted outlaw in the state!" Otto glared around the room, sucking on his pipe as his eyes danced from man to man. "Am I missing something?"

"It ain't right," Robin Cutler said. As the men's attention focused on him Cutler averted his gaze and looked around Otto's shoddy bachelor's space, but among the dirty clothes and plates and other such detritus covering the floor, he found no solace for his thoughts.

"What ain't?" Jerry asked.

"Any of it! Look-it where we are! None of this is right!" Otto exclaimed.

"I meant Cutler!" Jerry snapped. "I wanna know what he thinks ain't right!"

"You folks don't deserve this," Cutler stated.

"Sure, but when do folks ever get what they deserve in life?" Lou had been listening quietly, but he put this question forth for the group to ponder communally. "I mean, some folks have it easier, some folks have it harder, and unfortunately some folks don't seem to be blessed with any good luck all their lifelong days." Lou shrugged, unsure of how his statement would be received.

"It just ain't right," Cutler said, shaking his head but unable to bring up anything else for the group to ponder. His external silence, however, did not prevent his internal strife from preying upon his soul.

Thirty-Four

Even before he exited the two-storey home, Bug began to hide the noise of his boots on the stairs, tiptoeing down the naked planks and grimacing with every footfall.

The lower level was without candles, but once Bug pushed through the door and out into the night his heart froze, and he had to wait a panicked moment for his pupils to dilate before he could visually identify shapes in the dark. To his left was a clump of sage, and despite his overactive imagination, there was no Indian warrior crouching behind it. Bug began to breathe again, but the sound of the night concerned him, and he cupped his hands over his ears, realizing that the thundering sound he heard was not a stampede of horses approaching in the dark, but only his own heartbeat in his ears.

He tried to focus on slowing his breathing, but the night was much too oppressive to offer any relief. No matter where he looked, his eyes probed vigilantly for the demons he was responsible for defending against, but they could be anywhere! Bug felt his stomach knot and his bowels loosen and tighten alternately in sickening waves. His panic grew as he imagined passing out and being taken captive, asleep, and Aspirations' women and children all falling prey to Crooked's heathen hordes, with nobody else but Bug Calhoun to blame!

Bug fished out his paper sack from his back pocket and whipped it open, the brown paper crackling in the night. He looked about, conscious that he was attracting attention, then wobbled off to the side of the house to hyperventilate into the bag, like his mother had taught him to do.

Not a minute later and the side door to the two-storey home whipped open, and John Stakes strode out, then froze as his eyes fell upon Bug. Bug was leaning against the house but sliding downward while his legs wilted beneath him, and the bag pumped in and out in a series of desperate inhalations and exhalations, crackling like a smoker's lung as Bug fought to breathe into his paper sack.

"What's going on?" John demanded.

Bug shook his head and kept the bag pressed to his mouth, and John stepped forward impatiently and snatched the bag away.

"Hey! Speak up, boy!"

"I didn't (hurp)— I didn't (hurp), I haven't seen nothing! I'm sorry!"

John Stakes looked at the young man, and he knew that if he were to wash the dirt off of his face, he would not even find blond chin hairs underneath. John handed the bag back to Bug out of embarrassment, but Bug did not use it right away. He tried to breathe normally, but began to choke, and John knelt down beside him.

"I'm sorry. We're all just tense is all. The boys upstairs nearly shit their pants if you sneeze without announcing yourself first." John smiled at the boy, but Bug was still choking for breath, so John nudged his hands toward his face. "Use your bag, get breathing normal again. Then I'll give you a cigarette, it'll calm you down."

John stood up and stretched and looked off into the infinite heavens, staying with Bug until the paper bag was no longer needed. When Bug returned himself to a state of normal respiration, John invited him to smoke, and Bug took a couple of puffs, then stopped.

"Everything all right?" John Stakes inquired, hoping that

another episode of hyperventilation was not on its way.

"Can I, uh, is it wrong to save some for later?" Bug asked, referring to the half-smoked cigarette in his fingers.

John chuckled. "No. At yer age I'd pick up a trampled butt from the street and try to milk smoke out if it for two days before I gave it up. But you look cheap if you do it when yer older and can afford smokes. In my opinion you look weak too; women and young boys can finish a smoke easy enough, so unless yer brand new at it, then why's it taking you three sessions to finish?"

Bug nodded and took another puff but when he coughed John motioned for the cigarette. John set the smoke between his lips and pulled hard, the tip glowing furious red until it petered out and the smoke was finished. The nub that was left, John Stakes flicked off into the darkness without caring where it landed. Next John Stakes retrieved a fresh cigarette and a match and handed them both to Bug. "Here's a new one. Take your time, smoke it however you like and just enjoy. It's a nice night to sit out, and if you need anything we're upstairs."

John patted Bug on the shoulder then reentered the house where they were stationed.

"He okay?" Muttie Benson asked as John Stakes reentered the second-floor room.

"He's fine. There's nothing out there."

"He do something to piss you off?" Muttie asked.

John shook his head. "Bug's a good kid, he just got scared is all. Poor kid doesn't even smoke a whole cigarette at a time, but he's on watch against an outlaw, his criminals, and Lord knows how many wild Indians all banded together? It's McCleod that's pissing me off. I'm mad as hell and I mean to talk to him about it."

Thirty-Five

Crooked awoke before dawn. He crawled from his tent and pissed messily to one side of it, like a tripod on his knees with one hand in the sand, and he cursed the dribbles on his hand before he wiped them in the dry dirt around him, then resumed crawling along on his belly. Crooked dragged himself to his horse and lay in the sand to unhobble her, and the damned beast rose immediately upon being freed, so Crooked had to scale the side of the beast, as though climbing a fleshy tree. Crooked sat barebacked on his brown mare, and from this raised position he navigated his horse between the smoldering cookfires from the night before, searching for materials that he could use as crutches. A shoddy old Carbine Rifle, its stock wrapped in a padded strip cut from his sleeping roll, served as Crooked's first crutch, and the second came by way of a lance broken to length to match the rifle, and similarly outfitted with padding. But to watch Crooked locomote on his abominable, mismatching implements was pitiful. He battled every step, and his impaired balance and awkward gait only served to accentuate the malice he already felt toward his impairment.

But having acquired crutches, Crooked rode back to his tent and dismounted from his horse, in order to properly saddle the creature for the day. Crooked dismounted and cinched his saddle around the girth of his mount, then tied his barely serviceable crutches behind the saddle, before he swung up onto the back of the horse, propelling himself by the strength of his arms. Crooked mounted easily enough, but his pistol dropped from his holster and lay gleaming in the fresh light of dawn, taunting him where it lay in the sand.

"Don't dismount! Don't dismount, my good man, I am coming!" The cheerfulness rang out clearly, with little activity from the camp to compete with the voice, and so Crooked sat his horse and watched with cold eyes as Arthur Coe approached.

Coe walked over to the pistol, picked it up, and offered it helpfully up to Crooked Taylor. "I love the smell of ozone. Can you smell it this morning?" Crooked took his pistol without speaking, and Coe continued unabated. "When I awoke it was all that I could notice! It's like…" Coe paused and shifted his weight from one foot to the other as he thought. "It's like an electric charge in the air. It sits on your skin like humidity, it tingles your tongue with its metallic taste, it is the juncture where fate and the willpower of mankind come together; the might of providence itself, steered by the feebleness of humanity, and these twin and awesome powers, conspiring to create a single point in time, upon which the destiny of man hinges in its entirety." Coe closed his eyes and inspired a deep, dramatic breath through his nose.

"You talk too much," Crooked said. Coe smiled and watched Crooked stow the pistol he had fetched for him, and Coe kept his smile trained upon the crippled bandit, as he watched Crooked's brown mare raise sparkling dust across the white morning, riding toward Aspirations, Texas alone.

Thirty-Six

The walls of Troy had been dust for a thousand years, sediment upon the breeze, the once mighty foundations untraceable. Perhaps some of the dust once ground beneath the heel of Achilles' sandal, had travelled the world to be present at this event as well; to observe Crooked Taylor as he dismounted his unkempt pony, and leaned awkwardly against its slatted ribs, unstrapping his crutches from its flank.

Before him stood a wall of Aspirations' citizenry, their weapons as patchwork as their confidence. Quaking little boys and old men with out-of-date muskets, all of them wondering what their role in the standoff might be.

Crooked held onto his pony and seemed to be taking his time, when in reality he stood painfully on his lower limbs, cursing the knots he had tied to secure his crutches to the saddle.

All the world held its breath, and the sun shone so brightly that one could almost hear the dry grass baking in the sand. Crooked released his crutches, set them under his arms, then hobbled a couple of steps toward the assembled town, before he informed them all, of what it was he desired.

"Lionel McCleod!" Crooked shouted. No response. Silent moments ticked away, and Crooked surveyed the crowd with hatred, pure and irreconcilable. "Lionel McCleod! It's Bradley Taylor! Show yourself!" As Achilles had called for Hector, so too did Crooked Taylor demand that his counterpart produce himself, and that the two of them pursue their intertwined destiny, to its ultimate and preordained conclusion.

Thirty-Seven

He could feel their eyes. All of their gazes piled one on top of the next, their scrutiny more intense than the blaze of the sun. His neck buckled under the yoke of expectation; these people knew not the weight of what they asked. Lionel McCleod stood next to Father Jasper Calafort, and he could feel the urge within Calafort to confer with him; the desire of the priest to investigate his attitude, searching for the flicker of a martyr.

"Someone needs to go make sure everyone stays disciplined during this circus," McCleod said in an inflectionless monotone.

"What are you going to do?" Father Calafot asked, an undeniable twinge of hopefulness laced through his voice.

"Wait."

Calafort nodded and Crooked called out again.

"McCleod! I ain't going nowhere until you show yourself!"

The confidence of Aspirations' citizens was firmly attached to McCleod, but that confidence was not without its limits. Crooked would not stop calling for McCleod, and since no one else could answer to the fury of the crippled outlaw, it fell upon the major to determine what the fate of Aspirations would be.

"McCleod!"

Crooked Taylor stood propped up on his mismatched crutches, waving his pistols in the air, and he was so focused on producing a duel with McCleod, that when he let go of his horse's reins and it began to trot away, he did not bother to follow. The horse stopped to nibble a small tuft of straw-dry grass, coated with dust. The creature chewed happily, and because of its tenure in serving the outlaws, it did not even flinch when the shooting began. The stalks of its ears readjusted in the direction of the gunfire, but the pony's head remained bent, tugging at the stubborn roots of the vegetation it was eating.

Thirty-Eight

John Stakes was dozing, seated in a chair, and leaning against the wall, with his hat tilted down over his face, when Muttie Benson shouted from downstairs.

"John! John!"

John rolled sideways, upsetting the chair, and losing his hat in the movement as he bumped the upturned box serving as a table in front of him. The night's ashes, and their corresponding cigarette butts were tipped over, in addition to his empty tin cup, and his pistol.

"John!"

"Bug? Bug?"

John shouted for Bug before recognizing that it was Muttie's voice calling for him, and so he snatched up his pistol then raced out of Muttie's bedroom, rounding the banister and leaping down half the flight of stairs, and almost landing on Muttie as Muttie re-entered the house in a panic.

"Muttie, what the hell is the matter?"

Standing in the open doorway, a grizzled white man raised his repeater carbine to his shoulder. His eyes were focused on poor Muttie, having chased him into the house, and so the intruder shot Muttie in the back, cranked the lever of his Winchester, and followed it up with a second cataclysmic clap. Muttie was already hit by half a dozen arrows, but the gunshots would prove to be the fatal blow. Muttie fell against John Stakes while John Stakes pulled his pistol and shot around Muttie's collapsing form, dispatching the intruder with two shots to his chest. The intruder tumbled back against the wall, and his eyes were wide with surprise, but his hands were not without life. The intruder slid down the wall, staining it where he bled, but his hands fumbled to reorient his carbine, necessitating three more shots from John. The man tumbled backward with no more attempts at movement, when a cane arrow whistled through the open door, clattering against the banister. A second arrow embedded itself in the stairs just above John's right boot.

"I'm shot pretty bad, John," Muttie said.

John wrapped his arms around Muttie as the dying man made this moot observation, and he leapt backward, dragging the two of them out of range of the open doorway, and the projectiles that continued to pour into the house.

"Yeah, Muttie, it's not good," John Stakes said. He set Muttie down on the stairs, trying to be gentle but also expedient; "just hang on, gimme one minute." John stepped over the body of the dead intruder then kicked the man aside so he could lean his back against the wall and take up position, defending the open door.

Thirty-Nine

Bug's eyes snapped open, and he wondered if his nightmare had followed him into the daylight hours. His name was called a couple of times, and the urgency pulled Bug to his feet without boots or pants, and he ducked out of the room with his rifle, barefooted and clad in long johns, just in time to see John Stakes vanish down the staircase in a wild rush.

Bug turned and ran to the window where he saw a buckskin mare charging down the street, carrying a gruesome-looking man in an overcoat with a single-bore rifle of impressive size.

An arrow found the window frame beside Bug's head, and he leapt back against the wall away from the aperture, when explosions of gunplay announced themselves downstairs.

Bug was tempted to call out for John, but then he was shot. There came an explosion, and then the horrible stinging sensation of the pellets hitting his face. Bug was about to scream when he wiped his face and there was no blood, only wood chips from the shattered window frame.

The wood exploded again, forcing Bug further from the window as the whinnying of horses outside announced the arrival of more men, and though he had not actually been shot, the window bursting in his face was painful enough that he was both terrified and determined not to experience the genuine article.

Forty

"McCleod...! McCleod...! McCleod!" Gunshots sounded in the distance, interrupting Crooked Taylor as he leaned against his crutches and bellowed for McCleod. Upon hearing the gunshots Crooked's hands snatched his pistols. His hands were a blur, fluid like the strike of a cobra, and he held his pistols poised to strike with the black bores pointing at the citizens of Aspirations assembled before him.

"McCleod? What is this?"

Lionel McCleod, presented himself, but too late. The major solidified from within the crowd holding a Sharps carbine replete with telescopic lens, and the bark of the rifle answered Crooked Taylor's call.

At the sound of the rifle's report Crooked felt a terrible blow to his side, and the force of the impact spun him halfway around so that he was facing away from Aspirations when he collapsed to the ground. Crooked's makeshift crutches fell on top of his body, and he twisted from within the bleeding tangle of limbs and implements and pointed both of his pistols toward where McCleod's shot had originated. Crooked emptied all twelve shots in rapid succession, one explosion indecipherable from the next, as though the bullets were all stumbling over one another in a rush to be fired.

Ziggy Mars endured the worst of the storm, and he danced an epileptic jig, sprouting cherry blossoms from belly, neck, thigh, cheek, and thigh twice more, before he gave up the goat and fell dead.

No bullet found McCleod, but the gunfire from within the town of Aspirations intensified, and Ziggy's dance of death coupled with McCleod attempting a second shot — this one left a crater near Crooked's ankle — started the crowd into motion. The general assortment of action was chaos; no theme of organization or preplanning could be ascertained in the wild flight of Aspirations' citizens to gain cover.

Lionel McCleod led a small contingent toward the nearest available house; he set out with Martha and Edgar Munsch, Beaver Atkins, and Hannah Schneider in tow, but as the group dove one-by-one into the safety offered by the house, the absence of one of their members was noticed.

Edgar screamed, his voice insensible as he looked around the room and could not find his wife. "Martha! Martha!"

McCleod kicked the door of the house closed from where he lay, but not before he snatched a glimpse of Martha Munsch lying face down in the street. Beaver smartly rounded the dining room table, and setting his shoulder into it, shoved the table up against the closed door to buttress it against entry.

"Martha! Oh God, Martha is still out there! We have to go out there! I have to get my wife!"

"Hold him!" McCleod shouted.

Beaver looked at Edgar, Edgar at Beaver, and Beaver lunged for Edgar while Edgar grabbed the table and tried to wrestle it away from where it was jammed against the door.

It was the Munsch house that had been invaded, and so previously unnoticed, Edgar's twin daughters began to cry from the back doorway in which they stood, peering into the madness of the main room.

"Let me move the table! I'm going out there!"

McCleod stood up and grabbed Edgar from behind, wrapping his arms around his neck and constricting until Edgar's voice cut into a whispered wheeze. When Edgar's struggles abated similarly to his voice, Lionel McCleod released him and he stood gasping, while his daughters continued to wail in distress of what was going on around them.

McCleod picked up his rifle then stepped to the window, took a moment to sight his weapon, and then fired. The explosion was fantastic, shaking dust loose from the ceiling boards above, and prompting fresh cries from the Munsch twins.

"Whose kids are those? Shut them up!" McCleod snapped. Another deafening round clapped from McCleod's weapon, and the windowsill began to spit chips of wood as it attracted gunfire from without. "And I'll shoot whoever touches that table — you move it aside and you're signing a death warrant for us all." Another thunderous round took flight and Hannah groaned and cupped her hands over her ears, while Beaver stood, still hanging onto Edgar, and Edgar's hands still holding the edge of the table, but no longer pulling on it like before.

McCleod fired again, then dropped down below the windowsill and slid his Sharps carbine across the floor toward Hannah.

"Reload this!"

Hannah shook her head. "I don't know how!"

"Fine. Beaver, reload that!" McCleod shouted, motioning toward the rifle on the ground. McCleod fought with his pistol as he waited for the rifle to become available once more, and a horse screamed somewhere outside, while a downpour of lead began to exchange between Aspirations' buildings and the mass of bandits, rapidly approaching the city.

Forty-One

No sooner had John Stakes replaced the five spent cartridges in his pistol, than he leaned out the ragged doorway, and found himself face-to-face with a bandit that was entering through the same door. The two men nearly walked into one another, and each one adopted identical looks of bewilderment at their predicament. John raised his pistol more quickly than the bandit could raise his two-handed rifle, and John shot him in the face and the bandit fell dead beside his comrade in the doorway. A second man behind the first stood dumbly, looking down at the quick murder that had dispatched his comrade, then he turned to flee. John shot the second bandit twice in the back, and as he fell and lay groaning, John took a moment to secure his aim before he shot him for a third time, making sure that this round was final. The two bandits had courteously left their horses hitched to a nearby railing, and John ran toward the horse nearest to him, when his leg was swept out from under him, an errant shot catching him in the groin. John fell and he fired blindly, merely hoping that the shooter would have to take cover, as he struggled to his feet and waddled to the horse. John Stakes crawled into the saddle as the shooter, an Indian with the left half of his face painted red, and the right half charcoal-black, loomed out of a doorway across the road and fired again. John encouraged the man back into cover with the last round in his pistol, then spurred the horse to a gallop down the main avenue.

John's flight did not go unnoticed, and he cast a backward

glance over his shoulder while barbaric shouts were raised, and hoof falls accelerated after him. He slapped the horse, encouraging its flight, darkly aware that it would soon be obvious, whether or not he was out of range of his pursuers' rifles.

Forty-Two

With both pistols empty the full weight of his vulnerability settled upon him, and Crooked crawled across the sand like a frightened lizard, angling toward his horse. The crowd was slow to retaliate, distracted by the distant gunshots and their own innate disorganization, but there were no other targets about, and so Crooked Taylor's horse endured an abundance of gunshots, obliterating all hope of escape. Crooked crawled over top of the warm corpse of his horse and took cover behind its body, the stench of blood heavy in his nose, as he and the horse bled generously into the sand below. His shirt was damp, and his fingers were red and slick with blood, but even in such condition, they fed bullets into the empty cylinders of Crooked's pistol with enviable rapidity and smoothness.

But when he raised his head above the side of his horse, Crooked observed that the crowd had mostly been put to flight, save for one or two heroes standing their ground.

The reason for the dispersal of Aspirations' forces into the surrounding houses, was the terror incited in the souls of all of Aspirations, by the devil's jubilee racing across the desert sands toward them. One Indian riding near the lead wore a thick wool overcoat and had a gold pince-nez flapping from its chain like a bauble dangling from his vest. His face was painted red and black, and he had stuffed great feathers into a bowler hat which he held in place on his head with a strap beneath his chin. One white man's face was shaved but for great puffy mutton chops, and he rode upon a saddle impressed with sterling silver inlay, and a name and title that were not his own. It seemed he rode upon the entirety of his richness, because he had no rifle to fire, nor any pistol in his hand, but instead he waved an Indian lance, brandishing his traded artefact, as he barreled headlong into war. Like some great calcium wreck, Black Rattle rode across the plains, the bones upon his demon chariot clattering as he sighted down the long line of his Winchester repeater, toward the citizens scattering at their approach.

The people of Aspirations did not know what sins they had performed that required such grave punishment, but they were positive that this mendicant horde could only be former inhabitants of hell; Satan's selection of souls, sent back to earth for not yet having performed enough evil upon the world.

Forty-Three

The violence was rapid and difficult to decipher. Bug heard the crash of a pistol through the floorboards, multiple times in rapid succession, followed by another clap, a loud thud, then nothing. Bug strained his ears as he stood beside the window, clutching his rifle to his chest with bloodless fingers, while his Adam's apple bobbed, and his dry tongue kept getting stuck to his teeth and his lips. Bug's mouth formed the syllables 'John,' but there was no air to accompany these words. Bug longed for John Stakes' gruff reassurance that his fears were overblown, but he was paralyzed to call out, and felt like a fawn in the forest, separated from its mother.

Bug stood in the relative silence of Muttie Benson's upstairs room, and as the dust motes twirled in the sunlit air of the stuffy room, the more subtle details of his situation impressed themselves upon him. Bug listened to the muted gunfire of a city in turmoil. When horses whinnied nearby and their cries were interspersed with the shouts of men, Bug felt sick and thought he might pass out. He listened and wished for all the world that he was somewhere else, but eventually, he dredged up enough bravery to slink toward the window and lean out past the frame to take a peek. He pulled his head back as though it had been scalded, as Bug Calhoun had just spotted his first real-life Indian. But what he had briefly seen poorly matched the image Bug had formulated in his mind of what an Indian should be, and so he chanced a second look to make sure. The man was much shorter than expected; no taller than Bug himself. He was also skinny; the white lines of warpaint on his torso, accentuated the xylophone of his ribcage, and he wore a silk ascot around his neck, blotched with tobacco and whiskey stains. His shoes were traditional leather moccasins, but the leggings looked awkward pulled over the top of faded blue jeans. Bug watched as the little man trotted over to a body lying in the street. The man stooped and began to check the person's pockets for valuables, when Bug ducked back from the open window once more. From his own pocket the brown paper bag appeared, and Bug gripped its crumpled shell, as though it might still imbibe some comfort just from being held in his hand.

"John probably got away," he told himself. "That body ain't John. John got away. John's gone to get help." Bug repeated this continually like a mantra, but he felt the rising panic pushing him toward a bout of hyperventilation. He tried to calm himself, but could not remember what John Stakes was wearing, and if his clothing matched the dead man's whose pockets had just been emptied.

Bug gulped and tentatively grasped the paper bag, but as he began to peel it apart the paper's crackling sound made him freeze. Bug listened, but his breathing was all that he heard. Bug peeled the bag apart again, wincing at its noisiness, when the sound of boots on broken glass crackled in the house below him. Bug tucked the bag into his front pocket, picked up his rifle, then strode to the corner of the room where he sat down, made himself as small as he could, and propped his rifle against his bony shoulder. This time his ears were not deceiving him; the footsteps were multiple, inside the house, and heading for the stairs.

Forty-Four

As the first wave of heathens broke against the city, McCleod tossed weapons back and forth in a furious exchange with Beaver, because Beaver declared that McCleod's hand was a more efficient use of ammunition than his own. The bystanders could do nothing but cover their ears and observe the machinelike patience with which McCleod approached his work. Hunkered down in the elbow of the windowsill, McCleod kept both eyes open while firing, and he narrowed them like a bird of prey before squeezing the trigger in a smooth, almost tender motion. With the requisite force and no more, McCleod eased the oiled trigger through its range of motion, impervious to the sound of the gun as it awarded death to the unlucky souls located in its crosshairs.

The forward-most riders of the bandits broke in myriad directions upon reaching the city, alternately chasing citizens, and running for cover themselves, as the battle mounted in scale and intensity.

McCleod shot a bandit riding past on a horse, and the splash of red accompanying the shot told McCleod the bullet had found his lung. McCleod swung his rifle toward a new target, all the while ignoring the shivered bits of wood landing on his hat brim, as the windowsill exploded all around him. The lung-shot man leaned drunkenly to one side, and his weapons slipped out of his slackening hands, and he bowed over the horn of his saddle until he looked like a dead body; captured and tossed onto the horse like a trophy. Lacking direction, the horse stood, turning this way and that in the street, and the lung-shot man's eyes rolled as he batted his eyelids and tried to stay awake.

McCleod's second round targeted an outlaw taking cover behind a fence, and McCleod shot him beneath the shoulder blade, throwing him onto his knees. The man popped right back up, thought better of it, then crouched down to hold onto his kidney and die.

One could not tell from McCleod's face whether or not a round landed. He never rushed his shots, and he did not flinch in response to those firing at him. McCleod lacked any reaction to the shouts and screams and firing and running and bleeding and anger and desperation. He ticked away like a clock, sighting and firing, sighting and firing. McCleod kept perfect count of his bullets, and never dry-fired a trigger emptily. When the gun's ammunition was out, McCleod would toss it to Beaver then pick up one of the loaded weapons nearby, swing it up onto the windowsill, and return to his task as a purposeful, undeterrable mechanism of doom.

Beaver sweated into his eyes and his hat brim was moist, but he reloaded the various arms under his charge as quickly as he could without jamming them, because McCleod had already pronounced that their best chance of survival was to kill as many of the bandits as they could, before the enemy forces could organize themselves.

Forty-Five

McCleod's murderous efficiency, along with the steadfastness of a few pockets of citizens, slowed the criminal advance upon the city. And so, dissuaded by the volume of dead comrades filling the streets, the bandits began to turn back.

Evan Herndon of Evan's Metals leapt out from where he had been hiding in his bedroom, and gunned down two men in a surprise attack, but unfortunately a good number of criminals were within earshot. Evan's Metals was promptly invaded, and Aspirations' metalworks soon rang with screaming.

Black Rattle appeared on the balcony of Evan's Metals, and he looped a rawhide rope around the corpse of Evan Herndon, then tossed the recently skinned body over the railing to hang by the neck. Evan hung ten feet from the ground, suspended like a Peking duck in a market; a deterrent to all future heroics.

Black Rattle plucked two living torches from the metal holders hanging on the outside of Evan's Metals, and he cast these deep into the living quarters above the metal shop. Then he descended to the street and watched his men loot the metal shop for useful items down below, while gouts of blue smoke billowed from the living quarters above.

The buildings of Aspirations that were ablaze lent an evil red glow to the crimson tint of sunset, and multiple chimneys of charcoal smoke rose like gray pillars, propping up the clouds of heaven like a cathedral ceiling. Under this nefarious tableau,

Black Rattle returned to the bandits' camp like a conquering Caesar. His Hell-cart trundled, the bones behind cackling as they danced and tumbled together, while a small procession of prisoners followed behind, all of whom struggled mightily to avoid looking at the skeletons being dragged through the sand.

When Black Rattle came to a stop he leapt down from his cart and barked a few quick words of Comanche, ordering his men to tie up his prisoners for him.

Black Rattle found Arthur Coe sitting at his cookfire, already well into his meal, as the man seemed to refuse to alter the timing or quality of his dining experience for anything. The spread was meticulous, and Coe sat with a metal tray upon his knees, that supported two matching pearl white, bone china plates, the larger one holding the entrée (thickly sliced bacon), the smaller appetizers (cooked vegetables), and a matching teacup that steamed with the aroma of coffee. Coe possessed cutlery of equal quality; his large and small fork, teaspoon, tablespoon, and butter knife, all made of sterling silver, with a floral pattern etched into each of their respective handles.

As the heavy form of Black Rattle strode toward him, Coe held up one finger to signal that he needed a moment, and he exaggerated the chewing of his mouthful, until he swallowed and spoke. "Hello, Dark Rattle! I hope your day was both busy and fruitful!"

"Do you live to annoy people?" Black Rattle asked.

"Come, please take a seat, join me," Coe said, ignoring the inquiry.

Black Rattle was heavyset around his middle, but broad at the shoulders and thick through his wrists. But despite his mass, he dropped down into a cross-legged seated position, with an unexpected litheness considering his heft.

"Did you take any prisoners?" Black Rattle asked.

"No. None of my shots missed," Coe said. He grinned, then looked left and right, then found what he was searching for. Coe picked up a small leather wallet and tossed it to Black Rattle who opened it and looked inside. "All lefts. No cheating," Coe said.

The wallet was full of human ears of various ages, the newest additions red and nestled just on top, and as Arthur Coe attested, all of them were lefts.

While Black Rattle looked in the leather wallet, Arthur Coe leaned and grabbed a second bone china teacup, which he handed to Black Rattle and said, "Coffee?"

"Sure," Black Rattle agreed, setting down the wallet beside him.

"Good coffee?" Coe asked, producing a flask which he waggled above the two teacups.

"Make mine very good coffee," Black Rattle told him.

Forty-Six

Nobody offered Crooked Taylor a horse. None of the men moved to help him. The congregation of criminals watched pitilessly as Crooked crawled his way into their camp, dragging his legs behind him, and leaving little patches of red sand where his wet shirt touched the ground. Crooked's nails were broken and his palms chapped from crawling the eight hundred yards or so, from his mutilated horse, back to the campsite of Black Rattle, Arthur Coe, and their crewmen. Crooked crawled past Howard Orr and made a point of looking straight at him, but Howard could neither speak nor raise his eyes from the ground.

"You look good, Howard, being a traitor suits you," Crooked spat. A bank of white froth was built up in the corners of Crooked's mouth, and his skin was pale underneath the sheen of sweat that covered him all over. "Suits you real good." Howard stood, mute and dumb beneath the scrutiny of Crooked's ire, but Arthur Coe, his ever-present grin lighting his evil face, interrupted their conversation, addressing Crooked Taylor in his maddening singsong voice.

"Hey, Little Legs, where have you been all afternoon? I thought you would've been the first one back to camp!" Coe bent and stabbed two thick strips of bacon with his fork, retrieving them from within the sizzling pan over top of his cookfire. With the strips of steaming bacon upon a tin plate, Coe walked over to Crooked Taylor. "Although I must admit, when McCleod started the shooting so unexpectedly, I thought you might be done for.

All any of the rest of us could do was rush like wild dogs and hope we got there in time. But they must have had a good thirty seconds to let you have it."

"And yet they only got him once," Black Rattle interjected. "We'll never lose if they keep aiming like this."

"Exactly!" Coe agreed. He turned from Black Rattle and offered the plate of bacon to Crooked Taylor. "Here, Bradley, take this, it'll keep your strength up... I mean, so long as it doesn't just pop out of that hole in your side." Coe nodded to Crooked's wound, raising his eyebrows for emphasis, when Crooked slapped the plate and the bacon and tin tableware tumbled out of Coe's hand.

Coe donned a look of false mortification, and asked Crooked, "What's the matter? Were they too well done?"

"What are you doing?" Bradley croaked. His voice was weak, but his soul was teeming with hatred.

"Why I'm trying to prepare you for tomorrow, it ought to be another full day!"

"We can't just sit here, they're organizing themselves!" Crooked snarled.

Coe shrugged his shoulders. "What, do you think they'll learn to deal with hostages in the next hour? Let them try and organize," Coe said.

"Those are my hostages, Coe, not yours," Black Rattle reminded the man. "What you do to them, I do to you."

"Calm down, everybody, just relax," Coe said in the smooth voice of an experienced interlocutor. "I know they're not my hostages, I just wish I had thought of taking some, is all. A good idea is a good idea and deserves credit."

Black Rattle was wary as he looked upon Coe, but Coe seemed to have forgotten about the hostages, as he looked down at the twin strips of bacon lying in the sand. "Too bad, the bacon was quite good tonight." He picked up his plate and fork but left the bacon where it lay. Coe tossed the tin plate and fork he had offered to Crooked Taylor carelessly toward his other belongings, then sat down beside his ornate tray, and picked up his fork and knife to delicately resume eating his meal.

Forty-Seven

The hoofbeats of the horse thundered beneath him while the rushing of the wind whistled past his ears, and John Stakes hugged his horse's neck like a jockey, because every advantage counted. John could feel his pulse squirting from the wound in his thigh, but he had no time to hitch a tourniquet around the flow, because four riders were kicking dust in his wake.

John Stakes chanced a look behind, but the horse's gallop jostled his vision too much to see. A gun's report ruptured the silence upon the plains, and John winced in anticipation. The shot must have fallen wide, because the horse's gallop remained unaffected, though another peal of thunder suggested that the men were not done trying.

John Stakes' horse maintained its pace admirably, and two of the riders peeled away, each chancing a lucky shot with their long rifles, but neither landing anywhere near enough for John to mark their fall.

Now, with miles behind him and only two riders in tow, John Stakes crested one rise and then the next, but each time he looked back, the men behind him were beating their animals without mercy, in an attempt to overtake him.

The road was a white scar worn into the boundless face of the earth, and this ribbon of trodden ground continued past the horizon, its terminus lost beyond the ether of sunset's glow. With an endless road to travel laid out before him, John Stakes did not want to test the endurance of his mount against two horses, and their undeterrable riders.

John Stakes angled his mount off the beaten path, but he had travelled no more than one hundred yards when he began to regret the decision. The straight-line speed of his burly horse was like a locomotive having built up inertia, but the coarse, rocky footing, and intermittent patches of shrubbery, quickly took its toll.

John turned, slapping his horse's flanks, and saw that both riders, one white one Indian, had their rifles pressed to their shoulders in preparation to fire.

"Move goddammit!" John roared, slapping at his blood-wet thigh until he located his pistol, then drawing the weapon, angling it backward, and firing a flesh-wound into his own horse's rump. A small pucker coughed blood, and the horse broke its teeth on the bit as it screamed then clamped down, its jaws snapping open and closed like a turtle as its head waved back and forth.

A rifle cracked and the horse stumbled, and John fired twice in the air, sending the horse into an ever more desperate state of panic. The horse reared and John dropped his pistol and clung to the saddle horn as a bullet bit into the mad horse's belly, encouraging the beast to charge blindly forward. John no longer had control of the accelerating animal, and he simply hung on to it, in the hopes that its instincts could lead them to safety. But the frenzied animal was senseless in its flight. The horse crashed into a patch of chaparral where its front legs became entangled, and the horse cartwheeled over its limbs with a snapping sound, ejecting John Stakes from the saddle. Stars exploded as John landed, and the world heaved like the decks of a ship on rough seas, but he fought his way through this delirium, rising to his unsteady feet, and demanding that they run.

John's groin bled determinedly, and his right boot squelched with each footstep, leaving small red boot prints to mark each step.

Shots chased him, plumes of dirt leapt like miniature sand geysers all around him, and John pumped his arms as his vision swam. Behind him, and the horsemen had rounded the chaparral where John's horse lay thrashing, and they accelerated after the man, hobbling against his groin-shot injuries to flee.

Forty yards in front of John Stakes the earth dropped away; a shadowy split, marking some sort of canyon or arroyo. His head swiveled back and forth, from charging riders to chasm and back again, and John Stakes hoped that the gulch was wide enough that neither man nor horse could attempt the jump, although with the land so vacant and featureless, it really did not matter; the gulley was his only hope.

Bullets sparked on the stones like flint, and a shot to John's calf caused him to stumble, though he was close enough to this blessed fissure in the desert, that he hop-stepped over the edge, tossing himself out into the mercy of empty space.

Forty-Eight

A cache of guns was loaded, and situated beside Major Lionel McCleod as he stood smoking, and staring out the window of the Munsch residence, toward the congregation of bandits in the distance. Across the dark, unresolved plains McCleod could see the shadows of figures bandying about in the firelight, and others hollering with drunken shouts of victory. Female hostages were made to strip and dance, while children hostages served beverages to the crooks, and the congregation grew wild and loud, and their mirth decorated the prairies with laughter.

Inside the Munsch household, Edgar lost control of his grief again, and he began to cry loudly enough that Hannah felt compelled to hold him and shush his complaints while he wept about his wife. When McCleod could suffer no more of Edgar's weakness, he ordered that the house be searched for food and water.

"Edgar, make yourself useful. Gather whatever reserves of food and water you have, bring them to this main room here."

"What? Why? How long are we going to be here?" Edgar moaned.

"It isn't up to me," McCleod replied.

"But isn't there anything we can do?" Edgar begged.

"What would you like to do?" McCleod asked.

Edgar looked at the others, but they had no suggestions for him either. Eventually all of the occupants of the Munsch household settled their gaze upon Major McCleod for their salvation, just as McCleod knew they would. Outwardly, the major appeared to appreciate his cigarette while he stood by the window, but his internal attention had nothing to do with his cigarette; his focus was to stop his hand from shaking.

Forty-Nine

Few nights in the life of Bradley Taylor felt longer than the terminal period of lying beneath the stars, and feeling his life bleed out of him. He counted time according to the plugs of gauze he used to stopper up his wound, and by morning, he lay with a collection of crumpled ruby tissues, scattered in his vicinity. He must have slipped into unconsciousness at around dawn, because when he awoke next, the sun was white and stabbing to his eyes.

"Crooked... Hey, Crooked..." The fumbling orbs of his eyes rolled into place, and Crooked squinted to discern the person responsible for waking him up.

"Hey, Crooked, I brought you some water. Here."

Howard Orr set a waterskin down beside Crooked Taylor, then kindly stepped into the direct beam of the sun when he stood back up, offering Crooked some shade across his face so he might be able to see.

"Howard," Crooked said, smiling now that he recognized the man. "Are you wounded, Howard?"

"Wounded? No, sir."

"That's good. Be careful though. There's going to be lots of bullets flying."

"I brought you some water," Howard said.

"You know my feelings about shooting a man in the back," Crooked continued, ignoring what had been said by Howard. "But I'd be lying if I said that yours wasn't a tempting target. Be careful." Crooked pantomimed a pistol with his fingers which he pretended to fire, providing the accompanying sound with his mouth; "Pow."

"Crooked, I didn't—"

"No, I get it," Crooked snapped, silencing Howard. "I understand perfectly, you're taking care of your own skin. That's fine by me. It's only because you rode with me for so long that I'll do you the favor of telling you, I'm going to kill you, Howard."

"The hell you will," Howard spat. He stepped back and Crooked grinned as the sunlight hit his eyes, blinding him with tears as he continued to speak.

"I am going to kill you, Howard. But run along, go and whine to Master Coe. And when you do, tell him that I'm going to kill him too!" Crooked watched every step of Howard's retreat as the man scampered away, continually tossing nervous glances over his shoulder while he did so. Howard returned to one of a number of campfires where men were lounging, drinking, and throwing ruddy cards into a pile, playing for money that none of them yet possessed.

Fifty

The sides of the arroyo were steep, stony, and unforgiving, and John Stakes' lay twisted among the rocks at bottom, inventorying his body's pain, versus its ability to keep moving. The wound in his groin was like being branded by a hot iron, and his forearm throbbed in competition with his crashing skull, while a multitude of small scrapes and scratches decorated what was left of his clothing with blood stains. It was the noisy breathing of horses that alerted John to the presence of others, and the wounds in his groin, forearm, and scalp were forgotten as John Stakes crawled under an overhanging shelf of rock and curled his knees up to his chest so as to be hidden completely.

"Where'd he go?"

"He tossed himself over."

"I saw that. I mean where'd he go down there?"

"Go check."

"We shouldn't need to go check. Dead bodies are easy to find."

"Well, it ain't goddamn there!"

One of the men made the sound of hocking spit, and the horses snorted breathlessly from their exertions.

"Dammit. All right. You try that way; I'll try this one. Call if you find anything." The sound of the men and their horses dissipated over the course of a minute, until the air above the arroyo was once again hot and undisturbed.

John crawled out from under the rock, but as soon as he rose to stand, he had to bite the inside of his mouth to keep from screaming. He sat back down onto the ground and observed that the stain at his groin was oil-black from so much blood pulsing through the denim. He released his belt and tied a tourniquet, his head on a swivel, listening for the return of the horsemen, but the wound was too high up in his groin for the tourniquet to function. John abandoned the tourniquet, and with his wet belt slung around his neck, he rose carefully, and left his injured leg dragging as he began to hop from one stone to the next, praying with every landing that he didn't turn an ankle.

When the men returned John had barely enough time to drop to the ground and work himself into an alcove in the wall. John had not hopped far, he made perhaps thirty- or forty- yards progress on one leg, and though the men seemed to have returned to the spot where John Stakes originally fell, he was not far enough removed from them to feel safe.

"Anything?"

"..."

"Well?"

"Did I call you? No? Then that means I didn't find him!"

"We can't go back without his body. At least a scalp or an ear!"

"Are you donating?"

"You're in this just as much as me."

"I know. But we do not have to admit that we were part of the chase, people are forgetful."

"Are you nuts? Too many people saw us! Hugh, Whitney, Aho... how many others rode halfway out here with us?"

"Then we take flight. The north road is right here, I may just take this road and not look back."

"You can never come back this way again then. Not you or

your family neither."

"I know it."

"Plus, I forgot all my stuff back there. What do you have on you?"

"Nothing. But things can be replaced."

"Sure, but it can be unpleasant doing the replacing. I'm not riding off with only the clothes I'm wearing like some Indian… Not Indian from your tribe, one of the other ones I mean."

"You're a fool. Either we ride away right now, or we turn back and tell everyone that we found him and got rid of him."

"They'll ask for an ear at least."

"The horse he stole from us snapped its leg and we'll bring back the saddle and kit to prove it. We'll say he tossed himself down into that arroyo, and you and I shot him four or five times, then watched him for as long as it took us to smoke a couple of cigarettes, before we turned around and came back. He was lying in a big pool of blood and didn't move for a long time. We didn't climb down into the arroyo to get him, because we didn't feel like breaking our necks just to fetch a scalp or an ear. If anyone questions it, send them this way. They'll find the dead horse and the ruined chaparral, and if they fail to find the man's body, then we explain that the coyotes must have been quicker to find it than they were, that's all."

"I like that. And it lets us go back and get everything we need — plus a little extra if we see the chance — before we get outta there."

"The man is on foot. The closest town is Fort Chamberlain, and that's seventy, seventy-five miles from here. Say he meets someone on the road, what of it? We will have all of tonight to assemble what we can, and if things start to get sour, then we know to retreat early. We can remain at the fringes of the fight and be ready to go at a moment."

A gunshot barked.

John froze, craning his ears in a silent world that offered only the faraway trill of cicadas. It became quiet enough, that John was tempted to resume his travels, but his agonized patience was rewarded when a slide of dust exploded from the steep sides of the arroyo, and then a second, before a body landed heavily and unmoving on the chasm floor.

John waited for as long as his thinning patience permitted, counting to one hundred in his head twice, before he crawled out of cover and began to move once more.

"Keep going, John. Find somewhere you can climb, get out of this arroyo and keep going." It was sound advice, but when John Stakes looked up the sides of the arroyo his faith in the remaining function of his body was questioned, for his groin was still bleeding, each pulse-beat of blood, the ticking of a clock counting down.

Fifty-One

The sun's light was all but absent from the world when a congregation of bandits approached the outlaw camp. Both Coe and Black Rattle stood up from their extended, luxurious meal, while Crooked Taylor lay beneath his hat some distance removed but listening with great intent.

"What happened?"

"One of 'em shot Henry, hopped a horse and took off out of town."

"One of whom?"

"The folks here."

"Where is he?"

"Dead."

"So where is he?"

The answer provided was apparently silent, so Crooked had to roll his head to the side and peek out from under the brim of his hat, to ascertain the answer to Black Rattle's question. A wet flap of scalp lay curled in the dust at Black Rattle's feet.

"I rolled the body down a gully. About six of us chased after him all told, but I carried on alone. All the other horses were failing so I rode over ten miles chasing him down. He chose a good horse when he stole Henry's."

"Where is the horse?"

"The oaf rode Henry's horse straight into a big patch of chaparral and the horse flipped three, four times and broke its leg. Surprised the fall didn't bust the rider's head wide open, but he crawled out from under the horse and kept on running."

"He had some salt to him huh?"

"More salt than most of you slugs." There was laughter and bantering, and the man remained the center of the mob's attention for a time, but Crooked's interest waned, and he turned back toward the dark underside of his hat, closing his eyes, and holding out for morning.

Fifty-Two

As the night progressed about the bandit camp, grievances arose between small bands of fighters, most allegiances split along the lines of Arthur Coe's crew, versus the men of Black Rattle's. Black Rattle was quick to diffuse such spats, though his threats of violence seemed to have no effect, and it was not until he told the men that their claim to the bounty of Aspirations was forfeit, that their tempers would subside. Arthur Coe did nothing to quell the violence, even when it was imposed upon his own men. As Ricardo and Lawrence fought with knives, Coe stuck out his boot, tripping his own man Ricardo, and squealing with glee as Lawrence fell on top of him and proceeded to stab him two dozen times. Coe watched the mauling with his knees hugged to his chest to keep his boots out of the way of the slaughter. So disconcerting was Arthur Coe's attitude toward the men, that a potentially lethal brawl during a poker game was dismantled simply by Coe tilting his head to the side to watch. It was almost as though the inquisitiveness the men saw in that impish face, somehow foretold their own doom. The squabble ended with insults but nothing more.

Not long after the averted poker game massacre, Coe stood up from the fire he had been religiously tending all day and strode about the camp. No matter where their loyalty lay, the men's eyes could not help but follow Coe wherever he went. He cut a slender figure, his shoulders like bony knuckles in his shirt, and his neck was too thin for his head. He looked almost youthful as he inquired about men's evenings, acting as though he were strolling through some public part of town, and currying favor like a politician. So natural was Coe's walkabout that there was no issue raised when he walked near the captives. After their duties as servants had ended, the captives were retied, and the long rope joining them all together was augured into the ground by a series of posts, out front of the city, where Aspirations citizens could view them clearly.

"Good evening, darling, I love your hair," Coe said to a captive. He stopped in front of this woman, produced his pistol, then set the gun to the woman's temple and fired.

Hostages and bandits alike were equally shocked by Coe's behavior, and the whole silent congregation watched as the dead captive slowly leaned forward until she lay prone in the dust.

Black Rattle stood, but his voice was still too surprised to be angry.

"Coe?" he asked.

"Now, I know what you're thinking—"

"Coe, what are you doing? You dumb son of a whore!" Black Rattle began to stalk toward Coe, and the men around him unholstered their pistols, unsheathed their knives, and flocked to their leader like ravens. Coe stood his ground as Black Rattle and his men approached, though the look on his face appeared giddy instead of frightened.

"Listen, everyone, just hold on," Coe began.

"Coe, I told you," Black Rattle seethed. "I told you they're mine."

"Yes, I know, but if I would have suggested this, you would have argued, then it would have turned into a whole big issue. Better to beg forgiveness than to ask permission, yes?"

"No," Black Rattle said, pointing his colt dragoon at the center of Coe's slender chest. Coe scratched his forehead and watched impatiently. "Coe, you're a stupid son of a bitch. I told you not to touch them—"

"Yes, yes, I know," Coe interrupted. "I know that you want to shoot me, but if you do then my men will shoot you, and then your men will shoot my men for shooting you for shooting me, and thus to cut a long story short, everyone will get shot. However, I'm quite certain that the folks in Aspirations will have no objection if we start pulling triggers against one another."

"What is wrong with you?" Black Rattle asked.

Ignoring the question, Coe turned around to face Aspirations, and the invisible audience barricaded in their homes. "I count… Eight hostages left. Tomorrow morning, if we do not see a nice long line of surrendering citizens, I will shoot someone else. And the same will keep happening until you surrender." Coe turned back to Black Rattle. "This is how we speed things up. Now they know our threats are real, and I assure you, the burden of eight doomed souls will be too much for these citizens to resist; it will not take many hostages to enact a surrender."

It now fell upon Black Rattle to respond. He held the dragoon level at the smiling Coe, and only with great effort did he lower the weapon again.

"One day you will be attached to my cart. I will drag your skeleton until the bones are sanded away into nothing."

"When I am done with this body you have my permission to do so. But not until then," Coe replied. He looked around, scrutinizing the men by the orange wicker of firelight, and found nothing lethal within their eyes. "Anyways, now that that nasty business is behind us, I recommend that we set our weapons aside and return to our leisure." Coe nodded to Black Rattle, as though to signal the end of an official meeting, and then bid the men a good evening, as he retired for the night. "Goodnight, all. I will be in my tent if anyone needs me."

Crooked Taylor was not idle during the commotion created by Coe. At the height of the ruckus, Crooked rolled onto his belly and pulled himself along the ground until he reached a gunny sack left by one of the fires. He rooted through the supplies, procuring for himself a third pistol and a dozen or so shells, all of which he stuffed down into the baggy legs of his jeans. And as the scene came to its conclusion, Crooked crawled back to where he had been lying, laboriously obscuring his drag-marks by swishing his crutches back and forth in the disturbed sand, until he was returned to his former attitude of reclination.

Fifty-Three

Bouts of lightheadedness plagued John Stakes regularly, forcing him to sit and blink away the red and purple polka dots forming in the corners of his vision. Twice while searching for an accessible path up the side of the arroyo, he had to lie down because the whole world seemed to be slowly rotating. But a stretch of canyon wall less sheer than the vertical cliff faces around him eventually presented itself, and for fear of his failing strength, John knew that he could not forgo the opportunity.

Had the bandit remained and chosen this moment to shoot John, John Stakes would have harbored no ill will against the man, because the pain of dragging himself up the wall by his hands and one leg was so terrible. He could not climb the wall in one go and parked himself against a stringy acacia tree and tried to breathe through the pain radiating outward from the wound in his groin.

"C'mon, John, one more good surge and you're there," John Stakes whispered. The final stretch of wall was nearly vertical, and so John prepared his heart for what was to come, and then attacked the wall, clambering up all at once, and rolling out of the arroyo before the full effects of the pain could impact him.

As he lay, the earth pinwheeled above him, the orange fire of sunset mixing with the black ether of night, into a swirling vortex of disorientation. He spit up what little water was in his stomach, then wiped the perspiration from his brow and rose to unsteady feet.

All the world was vacant, a lifeless void in every direction. John Stakes had no idea how many miles he could conjure from his injured body, but he tried not to dwell on this thought as he started forward.

Fifty-Four

While Bradley slept, he hoped his wound would congeal enough that he would live to see morning. He did not intend to expire in his sleep, despite how comfortable the option would appear. Instead, he remembered his first meeting with Lionel McCleod, where the man rode into town on a handsome buckskin horse, the sterling silver trappings of his kit capturing every stray ray of sunlight. He cut a majestic form, young, hard-faced, and determined to prove his worth. He said so in his eyes, so focused that he never took to joking.

The rangers were led by a man named Lionel Church, a captain to McCleod's private. Lionel Church cut no impressive figure of his own; his belly overhung his pants, and his hair was a riot of black and gray wisps, carelessly piled up and stuffed under his hat. Church's slovenliness and the flippant manner in which he approached leadership resulted in the rangers looking to Angel Burso, Church's Sergeant and second-in-command for their directions.

Bradley could not know the purpose of the rangers in the hotel; their leader presented himself so comfortably, the young man believed the troupe to be vacationing at the place. And although Bradley's father would never admit to it, whores were not infrequent visitors to the back rooms of his hotel. The rangers took their turns; whoring, drinking, gambling, and most importantly paying; luxuriating in all of the amenities the hotel had to offer.

The hotel's increased activity encouraged young Bradley to take up his fiddle, and he walked out to his place beneath the shade of the oak tree, standing upon two legs, as perfect as any pair created by the Lord above. He walked, cantered, sauntered, shambled, strutted, and locomoted in every way taken for granted, positioning himself out in the courtyard for some post mealtime music, just after high noon.

Bradley tuned his fiddle by ear and looked up to the south wing of the hotel, where the young Ranger McCleod stood, shaded by the eaves of the building, smoke tumbling out from beneath the low-slung brim of his hat. The other rangers were not easily visible, for their laxity in vigilance resulted in them all wearing half of their uniforms; the pants with a mismatched shirt, the shirt unbuttoned entirely to show their sweaty chest and damp undershirt beneath. Hats were on some heads, absent from others, and one ranger was even walking around, looking for someone in a too-tight hat, as his fell below his ears when he set it on his head. The rangers mingled with the hotel's other patrons, and the crowd was happy and unbothered, and to buoy the gaiety and encourage generous tips, Bradley started his set with a jig that set the fattest ranger to stomping his foot and clapping…

Fifty-Five

Elijah and Elrod Buckner sat beneath a despondent moon, their spirits low — both in bottle and soul. They had a single bottle of whiskey between them, and Elijah held it toward the light of the moon so the dark liquid could be visualized, and therefore split evenly. They had not made a fire, because at a time when the bottle was fuller, Elrod had asked Elijah about Lonesome Star, the ferocious Comanche chiefess, and Elijah had told him he was a dolt and that her name was Morning Star, and that he would rather meet her than Black Rattle. This led to another disagreement. Several drinks and topics later, Star of the Morning was properly identified, and in remembering her name, the old argument about who was more fearsome, Star of the Morning or Black Rattle, brought the duo's attention full-circle, and saw them discussing the dark night and the dry, fireless camp they had made once again.

"We should've made a fire," Elrod grumbled.

"Too late for a fire now," Elijah said. The moon was low but not yet set, but neither brother thought of sleep, instead sitting together for a long and silent interval, both equally alone in their thoughts.

"I wonder what stops a wolf going south," Elrod finally pondered aloud.

"Huh?"

"I mean, we got wolves up here, Northern Mexico got wolves, why don't Southern Mexico got wolves?"

"What's this talk about wolves?"

"Just talk is all," Elrod defended. "I thought it and couldn't figure it out, so I thought I'd ask you."

"It's easy to figure out," Elijah stated. "Wolves like mountains and such. Not beaches and forest and god-awful desert."

"It's god-awful desert up here. Why's it worse down there? I dunno why wolves aren't straight down to Nicaragua or past that, in South America, and then all the way to the end of the world."

"It's the weather that stops them. Somewhere it's too hot and rainy so they don't go past that point. Like a dividing line."

"Yeah, but where? What makes that line where it is?"

"You hear that?" Elijah asked.

"Oh, quit it," Elrod snapped. "We already don't have a fire, you expec—"

"Shh!" Elijah said, punching his brother in the shoulder.

"Don't hit me!" Elrod said, swatting his brother.

"Elrod, shush!" Elijah exclaimed, punching his brother harder.

"Elij—"

"Honest to God I heard something."

The tone of Elijah's voice pierced his brother's inebriation, and Elrod shut his mouth, scrabbling about for a moment with his hands, before he hoisted his buffalo rifle to his shoulder. "Where'd you hear it?" he whispered.

Elijah located his belt on the ground beside where he sat, and he withdrew his pistol, but had to check if it was loaded. Elrod reacted to the click of the cylinder's mechanisms, and he hissed, "What, your gun ain't loaded?"

Elijah levelled the pistol out toward the inky darkness,

pulled back the hammer, and stated with moderate confidence, "I'm pretty sure it's loaded."

"So, we'll just find out when you shoot?"

The darkness hiccupped, just enough to quell the brothers' squabbling, and Elrod called out in a shaky voice, "Who's there? Anybody?"

Silence.

"Well, it sure is a stupid thing to do, sneaking up on ten men in the dark and not even announcing yourself," Elijah called out.

"Ten?" Elrod whispered.

"If we can't see them, they can't see us."

"I need help!" Croaking out from the night, a voice cried out that sounded like material tearing, forming syllables within this rasp. "Help me, I'm shot, I need help."

The voice was accompanied by a rustling sound, not too far distant from where Elijah and Elrod sat.

"Elrod, what do we do?" Elijah whispered, quaking as he tried to hold his pistol steady.

Elrod fared no better, the muzzle of his rifle jittery as though it were a branch in the wind, and he replied, "Check if yer loaded."

Elijah angled his pistol upward, trying to capture an errant moonbeam in his pistol's cylinders to see if any of them held bullets.

But the shuffling sound snapped Elijah's pistol down from the heavens and he and his brother held their weapons trained upon John Stakes as the injured man hobbled toward them.

John's head lolled with his awkward stride and his spine drooped as though his torso was too heavy for him to carry. Both of John's arms were red to the elbow, and his right side was blood from groin to boot, with every step resulting in a squirt of blood, pulsing out from between the stitching of the boot leather. John Stakes dropped to his knees and began to blather while Elrod continued to scan for danger.

"Give the man a hand, Elijah," Elrod said.

Elijah tossed his pistol toward his kit, heedless of where it landed, and Elrod winced and jumped. "Jesus, man, what if it went off?"

"It might not be loaded."

"But it might be!"

If Elijah had been within reach, Elrod would have struck his brother, but instead he maintained his vigilance, aiming his rifle out into the night, while Elijah tended to their unexpected visitor.

Fifty-Six

A clapping sound woke Crooked from his frightful subconscious, and he opened his eyes to an iron sky, too dark yet for clouds to be visible. A gray form interrupted the surrounding stillness, a solitary and slender shadow in the pre-dawn murk. Bradley rolled onto his side and then his breath caught in his throat, the pain in his stomach reminding him why he had not moved the whole night through. When Crooked's anguish subsided, he focused again on the slender figure of Arthur Coe, toiling away out front of the city of Aspirations. From where Crooked lay, Coe appeared to be standing in the dooryard of the first house of the city — well within range of anyone with a firearm, and a tempting shot for anyone who knew the man's character. He dug with a shovel, not slowly, not quickly, but in perfect measured rhythm, as though he already knew how many strokes it would take to accomplish his task. Coe maintained this pace until he finished digging, and then he swung the shovel over his shoulder and returned to camp. Crooked pretended to be asleep as he observed Coe, but Arthur Coe did nothing spectacular. He returned to his campsite, set down the shovel he had used to dig, and then went over to the captives, where he picked up the post from the woman he had killed the night before. He pulled the post free of her body, then walked the post to the new hole he had dug, front and center for the city to see. Crooked quit watching as Coe anchored the post into its new hole, and closed his eyes, wishing for some reprieve from his torment before the day began.

Fifty-Seven

The sun dawned as though it were any other day. For Bug, the coming of the sun released him from a night-long paralysis, so that for the first time in hours he possessed the courage to sneak into the other room and relieve his aching bladder. He returned to his post at the window, thankful that the dam of his bladder had held until daylight. He sat and sighed, and felt lighter, if not entirely safe.

Fifty-Eight

Coe waited for full sun-up before stoking his fire to a rich orange blaze. Then, once he was satisfied with the flames, he retrieved the polished cooking utensils he had cleaned so meticulously the night before. Coe set a pan to frying five eggs, and in another he added a fistful of bacon grease, which he allowed to melt and bubble before he laid two thick strips of ham into the pan. The ham began to spit and curl as it cooked, and while it did so, Arthur Coe sliced potatoes, allowing each sliver to fall into the sizzling pan below. Coe proceeded to dice half an onion, a clove of garlic, then produced a hard knob of cheese which he sliced so thinly, that as soon as the shavings landed atop the crisping potatoes, they began to liquify instantly.

Coe finished his meal to the last bite and washed it down with a cauldron-sized pot of coffee. However, throughout his breakfast Coe remained alone, not sharing a word with anyone. Somehow Coe's men knew to stay clear, for the whole camp was only too aware of the post freshly erected near the town.

But questions were reserved for the ranks of the men, and the maestro ate his breakfast alone and at his leisure. Arthur Coe ensured that every aspect of breakfast was attended to, and that every stain was wiped clean from all of his cookware, before taking a seat atop his saddle which lay on the ground, stretching out his legs, and rolling a cigarette. Arthur Coe smoked the cigarette to completion then stood, dropped it, and crunched the ember beneath his boot. He took a brief trip to his saddle bag and retrieved something that he stuffed into his pocket, before leisurely strolling out beyond the camp, toward the new post in front of town.

Fifty-Nine

John Stakes lamented that the bonds of soul and man could be so unbreakable when all he felt was pain. His consciousness reeled, and his dreams blurred with the drunken slur of reality, and when he spoke, a many-headed Gorgon laughed and taunted him in a strange and alien tongue.

Devils danced upon brimstone, glowing orange, and they dashed ice water across his back, while little spiders pranced atop his scalp with barbed feet. John screamed and a horrible thumping tossed him into the air chaotically, and he tried to situate his head upon his shoulders but found it impossible, as he was too dizzy to determine which way was up.

And then pain. From his fingertips to the frayed edges of his toenails, all of it quit his limbs and centralized into his groin and exploded outward in a dolorous hurricane.

John Stakes coughed and when hot bile lashed his throat, he tried to move but was restrained. The pain again, tears stung his eyes and then dripped and were snatched away by the wind. John Stakes opened his eyes and blinked, trying to sort sky, ground, sky, ground, sky, ground into separate entities, until a third pain made the bile return, then project powerfully outward. John vomited, slouching in front of Elrod Buckner, and his puke splashed across the dappled mane of the brown and white pony.

"God, man! Have some manners!" John's brain seemed to be rattling around like a bullet in a bucket, but Elrod's powerful grasp kept him from leaning too far one way or the other and falling out of the saddle. "I'm sorry about the thumb trick, but you were looking green on me!"

The voice howled close to John's ear, and he shook his head and the streaming wind and the rolling gallop of the horse beneath him begged the question: why were they going so fast?

John turned and behind Elrod's shoulder, a thirty-Indian war party stretched out across the ash-white plains. Feathers and leather flapped and unfolded in elegant strides, and a cloud of dust rose like smoke from the trampled ground they left behind them.

"Don't worry, Elijah's fine!" Elrod roared. "He peeled off to the north about three miles back! They didn't fall for it though! Seems like you're the one they're interested in!"

John Stakes looked behind him again to try and fit the pieces of his dreams into this bewildering reality and Elrod laughed.

"Don't you worry, they ain't gonna catch us! Elijah may not be the fastest sprinter, but he can carry this pace all day! We could load three more of you on top and he wouldn't notice!"

John wondered how Elrod's brother's sprinting speed factored into their escape, but he then realized that it was likely that Elijah was the name of Elrod's horse, as well as the name of his brother. He wondered if Elijah's horse was named Elrod, and he thought that this was funny, and then his dreams snatched the world away and he tumbled down into unreality once again.

Sixty

Coe stood in the center of the stage of his own creation. Pistols at his hips, hair combed, hat set neatly on top, Arthur Coe was ready for his day.

"Good morning, Aspirations—"

"Hold on!" Black Rattle interrupted. Black Rattle had situated his wagon such that its bed was facing Coe, and he sat on the floorboards with his feet dangling just above the dust, his rifle across on his lap. After such a period of preparation, Black Rattle's interruption caused Arthur's Coe's face to curl into a rictus of anger before he could correct it again.

"Black Rattle—"

"Coe, you better tell me exactly what you intend to do with *my* hostages."

"If you'd let me explain—"

"No. No explanations. If you want one, tell me your terms of reimbursement."

Coe's eyes narrowed and the muscles at the angle of his jaw pulsed, but one could almost see these traits dissipate as he quickly regained his former composure. "Yes... Yes, I suppose you're right... And your timing could not be better, in fact..." Ever the showman, Coe left his statement unfinished. With the eyes of the bandit camp upon him, Arthur Coe reached into his pocket and produced a coiled length of whip, on the end of which three small fish hooks were attached. Coe uncoiled the whip and let the fish hooks dangle, mesmerizing in their pendular motion, flashing in the sun intermittently.

"I would love to know how you value your captives, Black Rattle!" Coe declared. Coe walked past the woman he had killed the day previous, and she lay untouched; even the buzzards knew to keep their distance. Only the flies leapt, circled about, then re-landed as Coe walked past the woman toward the next hostage. "Are they meat sold by the pound?" Coe stopped and surveyed the skinny form of Heather Lasker. "Because this one is lean, but she looks to me like she could last. Will you cut me a deal?"

"Coe—"

Arthur Coe's voice grew louder, and he ignored Black Rattle's protests as he stomped to the next post and snatched little Benjamin by his dirty shirt. "Or age? Do you charge by the year? Because in terms of utility, this one, what's he five? Nice and cheap! But I have found in my experience, there is nothing more powerful than the screams of a child to make adults lose their minds and surrender!"

Without warning Coe swung his malicious instrument and raked Benjamin's shirt apart. Blood welled up quickly, but the blow caused more fear than actual harm to the boy.

"Or is it gallons of blood that you're interested in? Black Rattle, do you charge by the pint?"

Black Rattle stood up in the back of his wagon and raised his rifle to his shoulder as he called for Coe to desist. "Touch another one and I'm firing!"

Near the back of the congregation Crooked cursed his unpreparedness, and piled his firearms into his lap, then began dragging himself by his hands toward the periphery of the assembled outlaws. Crooked heard the frightened cries of the little boy tied to the post, in between Black Rattle's rising animosity toward Arthur Coe, while every movement caused his wound to flare and make him dizzy.

"Coe, goddammit—"

"How do you appraise such fine merchandise? Tell me so we can settle on a deal, fair for the buyer and seller alike!"

Coe swung his terrible device at another victim, prompting a scream, and though Black Rattle threatened mightily, Arthur Coe danced an erratic path between the posts, zigging and zagging so that he never presented himself as a clear shot, continuing in his singsong voice all the while. "What is it that you prize in a victim, Black Rattle? What traits make them valuable in your eyes? Could it be volume?" Coe swung his whip, another child screamed, and Black Rattle hopped down from his wagon, his eyes focused down the length of his rifle scope, but still unable to fire.

Crooked looked at the cluster of outlaws, toward his horse, then back to the outlaws as he came to a decision. "Howard! Hey, Howard! Get over here you son of a bitch!"

Screaming filled the background, but it was late enough in the morning that Howard was drunk and obedient, and he ambled over to his former leader as Crooked picked up a pistol, cocked it, then shot off the top of Howard's head in a spray of gore.

Sixty-One

When Elijah entered the one-bedroom hospital building, he found Elrod pacing the small corridor outside of the room. "How is he?" Elijah asked.

"Oh, swell. Fine. In fact, when I left, he was sitting up and playing cards and thought he might join us at the dance tonight." Elrod followed this up with a punch to his brother's shoulder. "Would I be pacing if all was well and good?"

"All right. Fine. Do you remember them Indians?"

"Course I remember 'em! How could I forget?" Elrod hit Elijah again and Elijah returned the favor and said, "Well don't punch me, dummy! They caught up with me!"

"What?"

"Elrod got hung up on a fence. His big gut didn't clear it and he took out the whole railing, tripping up his back legs. Lucky, I got tossed or he mighta rolled on me."

"So, they caught you?"

"You deaf?" Another flurry of punches was exchanged, then Elijah continued his explanation. "They caught me cause they're friendly, idiot! Them Indians were Kiowa! They were chasing us because we rode right past this goddam Fort whatsit— they were trying to get us to turn around!"

Elrod's eyes billowed with recognition and then he closed them. "Oh God."

"It's not your fault."

Elrod shook his head. "Some of it is. I thought the map was

wrong or something. Damn. Damn. How many extra hours did I make him sit in the saddle?" Elrod kicked the wall with the toe of his boot and shook his head. "If that don't make a guy feel guilty, nothing will."

Elijah patted Elrod's shoulder and nodded, then tried to redirect the conversation. "You meet the doctor yet? He any good?"

Elrod shrugged his shoulders. "Chinese fella. Can't hardly understand a word he says but when I got here, they told me no one's better with bullet wounds. He visits all over the place, spends lots of time in Aspirations, down in Mexico too."

"I suppose they wouldn't use a weird little yella fella unless he's good," Elijah concluded.

"I hope not, 'cause I sure would like to see John pull through."

Sixty-Two

McCleod stood, hard and resolute as he stared out of the window. He heard the shouts of the victims, he heard the voices in his head, and the people in the house were urging him to fire.

"McCleod, you have to fire!"

"If I shoot then they'll know where we are! You wanna be hitched up to that post! Do you know what they'll do to you?" His rage frightened the house's occupants into silence, but when McCleod turned back to the window it was Edgar who spoke.

"Maybe you're afraid of what they'll do to you."

"What did you say?" McCleod turned.

"My wife is lying out there and I know if she was tied to that post, you'd still be shouting for us to keep our heads! Keep our heads for what? If you're not gonna use that gun, then give it here!" Edgar stood, but for all of his bluster when McCleod stepped toward him, Edgar took a step backward.

"I'm your best chance out of here. And they're not doomed, we can still—" The shooting started, and the disagreement was forgotten as McCleod ran back to his station at the window.

Sixty-Three

With the loss of his skull, Howard Orr's body teetered lifelessly, but before it even had a chance to collapse, Crooked fired three shots in the direction of Arthur Coe. Crooked saw one bullet strike Coe in the thigh, causing the showman to stumble, before Howard's body finally quit its feet. The pain in Crooked's wound exploded as Howard's corpse landed on him; stars circled his vision, and a terrible sensation of vertigo tilted the world this way and that, as Crooked blinked and shook his head and tried to return to the scene of his own creation.

Arthur Coe leapt behind a hostage and fired a shot at Black Rattle, whom he believed to be responsible for shooting him. Black Rattle hopped back up into his wagon bed, vaulting over the piles of crates and sacking, to hunker down behind this improvised shelter. Black Rattle did not waste time, and he sat up a moment later, directing fire at Arthur Coe.

Kutna, who had chased John Stakes into the arroyo, buried his tomahawk into the neck of a Sioux loyal to Coe, and the man fell to his knees and made excellent cover for Kutna as he pulled out his pistol and shot his next adversary in the belly.

From this moment onward, single shots and solitary acts of violence could no longer be discerned. The pent-up hostility between parties was vented all at once, producing a bedlam of violence in every direction, a mass hysteria that was accelerating beyond all realms of control.

Sixty-Four

McCleod watched as the mass of bandits assembled beyond the city descended into civil war, but he did not watch for long.

"This is our chance, let's go!" he growled. McCleod attacked the table and chairs against the door, scattering the barrier left and right until there was enough space for him to squeeze out the door.

Major Lionel McCleod shot three men in the chest in quick succession, levering bullets into the chamber with wicked rapidity, before he found Arthur Coe and loosed a shot in his direction.

Coe was hunkered behind a group of hostages, firing wildly as he shouted for someone to bring him a horse.

McCleod took an extra moment to sight his rifle, centering the cross hairs on Arthur Coe's sternum, when McCleod's arm chucked backward, and his rifle drooped toward the ground. The ripping pain of the bullet wound was like an aftershock, and Lionel McCleod staggered, searching the scene before him for the offender. A second bullet struck McCleod's foot, and he stumbled, then abandoned the search, limping toward a low wall to take cover. Beaver and Edgar followed McCleod out of the house, shouting after him that he had forgotten to hand them out guns.

"McCleod! McCleod, we ain't got no weapons!" Beaver braved the fray, and he left the cover of Edgar's doorway, sprinting to join McCleod at the low wall. As he crossed the dooryard, Beaver got shot in the stomach. Beaver doubled over but kept running, and a second bullet clipped him in the side before he threw himself to the ground and slid to a stop beside McCleod.

"Edgar!" McCleod called.

Instead of joining them, Edgar shook his head then ducked back into his house behind the door, looking out at the two of them from safety.

"Beaver, throw Edgar the guns you need."

"What?"

Chips of cement rained down on the brims of McCleod and Beaver's hats as they hunched down as small as they could and conferred.

"I'll hold them here; take the guns you need and throw them to Edgar."

"Throw 'em?"

"Just throw them across!" McCleod bellowed. He unslung one of the rifles on his shoulder and handed it to Beaver, and Beaver turned and threw the gun, but it failed to make the house, landing instead in no man's land.

"Goddammit, Beaver, we need that!" McCleod shouted.

"I can't throw," Beaver said, holding his stomach wounds with one hand.

"Then run!"

Beaver nodded upon receiving the orders, then steeled himself for another jaunt into no man's land. He rose in a crouch but no sooner had Beaver's hat breached the height of the wall than a bullet sent it cartwheeling from his head, killing Beaver instantly as it did so.

"Edgar, get the gun!" McCleod shouted.

Edgar looked at Beaver where he lay, then shook his head,

retreating further from the half-open door of the house.

"Goddammit... Goddammit," McCleod cursed. He slid another of the loaded guns from his shoulder, then waited for a lull in the firing before chancing a look over the wall.

The day consisted of gunfire and sunlight, a dusty pandemonium, but as the scene revealed itself, Major Lionel McCleod discovered a mounted Crooked Taylor bearing down on him, reins clamped in his snarling teeth, both of his pistols drawn.

Sixty-Five

"Ho! Father, hold up!" Moses called.

The burly priest pulled hard on the reins of his horse and, following his example, the congregation decelerated.

"What do you see, Moses?"

Moses squinted hard, and the dust produced by their horses crept up on the group like smoke.

"I saw it again. A twinkle of something silver."

"Where? What're you looking at?" Mark asked, staring off in the same direction.

"What did you see, Moses?" Calafort interjected.

"I told you! A twinkle of silver!" Moses snapped; his voice exasperated. "I stopped and told you all as soon as I saw it, I don't know more than that!"

All eyes looked to Calafort, but he turned around in his saddle, looking in the opposite direction.

"Moses, can you see any of the others behind us?"

Moses turned around similarly and added his hand to the brim of his hat, as though the extra shade would extend his vision. "They're still a piece behind us yet. Should we wait?"

"Crooked's wounded, at least once," Ed chimed in. "I say we keep going."

Calafort ignored Ed and said, "I think we should wait here. It doesn't make sense to proceed and get somebody hurt when we have reinforcements a short wait behind us. We should be safe here. Moses, your vision is twice what any rifle can shoot—"

"It's the only reason I keep the old bugger around," Clarita announced, though the group ignored her comment as they were too anxious to feign lightheartedness.

"How many wounds does he have?" Ed asked no one in particular.

"Two," Calafort said, keeping his eyes focused on the faraway cluster of citizens.

"McCleod get him the second time?" Ed wondered.

"No. Coe did."

Ed looked off in the direction of the silver that had halted them but was too far away for him to see. "Well, McCleod did enough that he's in rough shape. Two bullet wounds plus two days out in the desert? I doubt we find more than bones."

"Doesn't take much energy to pull a trigger," Clarita informed.

"Fine, but it's not like our triggers are any harder to pull! We're treating him like he's invincible!" Ed waited for a response, but when no response was forthcoming, he waved his hand to indicate that he was giving up with his questions.

It seemed a good time to dismount, so without saying a word Mark swung down from his saddle and landed with a puff of dust. He began to kick his legs and massage his thighs in an attempt to return some life to his saddle-weary limbs, prompting the other riders in his party to follow suit. "Might as well," Ed announced. Ed dismounted and conducted his own awkward jig to shake out the knots in his legs.

Within minutes of dismounting the riders assembled in a circle, sitting atop their bedrolls as they sipped water from their canteens, or rolled cigarettes. With their impromptu campsite in place, Father Calafort said to the group, "Ed, are you and Mark still interested in hearing about the rest of Aspirations' siege?"

"Of course!" Ed responded, while Mark uncrossed his legs and leaned forward intently.

"It got so crazy out there I couldn't tell who was shooting who," Clarita said. "We sorted them all out afterwards, but that wasn't until later."

Clarita looked toward Father Calafort as though handing the story back to him, but Father Calafort was no longer focused on the group.

"Moses? Anything?"

"Nothing. No movement, Father."

"How about the riders behind us?"

"Behind us?" Moses turned around, took his bearings then said, "They're coming, but not quickly. We might have a while to wait yet."

"Then we might as well hear about the siege," Ed said, inviting Calafort to return to the topic of interest.

Sixty-Six

Crooked felt Howard's corpse rattling on top of him from the impact of various gunshots, and he lay immobile while the world around him went mad. Horses weaved back and forth screaming with fright, the air was heavy with gun smoke, and the ground was accumulating bodies at a rapid pace.

The second sincere volley from Aspirations' citizens hit the bandits like a wave, dropping four of them immediately, and sending no less than seven others, hobbling away, cursing mightily as they gripped their injured arms, legs, shoulders and bellies.

Crooked fought free from beneath Howard's corpse, rolling onto his belly with a pistol in each hand, and pulling himself forward with his arms alone.

Crooked's goal was a horse whose owner had not even unhobbled the poor creature after the fight began. Petrified and without the free use of its legs, the horse had fallen, and now lay like a trout, kicking and screaming as it flopped about to no avail.

Crooked was not the only man angling toward this horse, and as Crooked saw the bandit approach, he stopped crawling, took aim, then shot the man twice in the chest to make sure he did not take the mount.

Crooked ceased firing and resumed his crawl when a bullet slammed into his side. Crooked shivered from the impact, and a deep and foreboding sickness threatened to overtake him, when he located Arthur Coe. Arthur Coe was using a dead man as a shield, holding onto him from behind with a tight embrace as he fired from behind his grisly protection. Coe's pistol was aimed at Crooked, and Crooked met Arthur Coe's gaze across the savage battleground, but Coe did not fire, and instead he dropped his pistol and furiously began to feed rounds into the empty cylinder. Crooked checked his guns to see that he was also out.

Coe had the lead, having already fed four rounds into his pistol, so he snapped it shut and located Crooked again across the field of battle, while Crooked had only enough time to pop open one pistol and slide a single bullet into the chamber.

Coe's first round puffed in the dirt beside Crooked, and Crooked fought the urge to flinch, focusing instead on a true and steady aim at Arthur Coe.

Coe's second shot burrowed into the dirt, inches from Crooked's torso, and his third smashed into Crooked's left hand, bursting the knuckles upon impact.

Despite this, Crooked's shot struck Arthur Coe in the throat, and Coe dropped the dead hostage he was holding and clapped his hand over the gushing wound. Coe reeled drunkenly on his feet, and his fourth and final shot erupted without any sense of being aimed, while Crooked used his mangled hand to flop open the cylinder of his gun and insert three rounds into the cylinder with almost the same speed as if he had had both of his hands available. He closed the cylinder with his chin and when he looked at Coe again, Coe was leaning against his wooden post, the front of his shirt a bib of gore. But Crooked could not be dissuaded, and so he fired all three of his bullets in a tight cluster, erasing Arthur Coe's head from above his lower jaw. The body of Arthur Coe stood headless against the post, and even managed what appeared to be a forward step, before it collapsed for good.

Crooked resumed his crawl, and when he arrived at the

downed horse, he slipped his knife free of his pocket and slashed the cords binding the animal's forelegs. The terrified horse scampered to its feet in a whirl of dust, and Crooked held tight to its mane as it did so, rising from the ground in tandem with the frantic animal, and riding it bareback as the horse accelerated toward a gallop.

Sixty-Seven

As the horse and rider charged, Lionel McCleod shot the man just under his collarbone, and the impact threw the rider from the saddle. The horse leaped over the low wall, but the rider was still attached to his mount by the stirrup, and the rider's impact with the low wall stopped the horse's forward progress. The horse whinnied and began to run lengthwise along the wall, its saddle lopsided as it dragged the man by his foot along the other side.

McCleod ran to grab the horse's reins, holding tight against the horse's thrashings as it tried to break free. McCleod fought the horse into a semblance of sanity, then peered over the wall to find out that the dead man attached to the saddle was not Crooked Bradley Taylor.

Regardless, the man was firmly attached by his foot, and McCleod cussed as he tried to remove the foot from the stirrup. A bullet caught his mount in the flank, and it reared. Between McCleod's efforts and the horse's sudden movement, the mangled foot twisted free.

The horse could not be tamed; it reared and screamed and thrashed its head, but despite its terror, McCleod swung himself up into the saddle and whirled the horse around with a violent tug on its reins.

The battle had reached its crescendo, pandemonium reigned in all directions, and among the sunlight and dust and gun smoke, it became nearly impossible to discern friend from foe. But it seemed that there was no escaping destiny, and somehow within this maelstrom, Crooked Bradley Taylor and Major Lionel McCleod located one another. It is said that the last view of them during the height of the siege, was the sight of a brown horse carrying a wounded Crooked Bradley Taylor, galloping westward, with Major Lionel McCleod following in close pursuit.

Sixty-Eight

Outside the hospital some terrible commotion was occurring, and Elrod leaned out the window and scowled, wondering how decent people could make such a racket next to a dying man.

"They should have some respect," Elrod muttered to himself.

"They're getting ready for war in Aspirations, they're bound to make a little noise," Elijah said.

"How much noise does it take to load a gun?" Elrod pouted.

Elrod's temptation to say something to the crowd outside was growing, but when Doctor Chen exited John Stakes' room, both brothers' attention was entirely focused on the slender physician.

"Well?" Elrod asked.

"I could not stop the bleeding, his insides are torn. I tried to sew him together, but it was too late."

Elrod looked at his brother. "Could you understand a damn word he said?"

"Nope," Elijah said, shaking his head.

Doctor Chen rolled his eyes and shook his head in frustration, then delivered a diagnosis that even Elrod and Elijah could not misinterpret. "Alive... No." Doctor Chen shook his head. "Dead... Yes." Doctor Chen nodded. "No time..." he emphasized this by slapping the breast pocket where he kept his pocket watch. "More time, maybe he would have lived. There was not enough time, so he died."

"All right! All right I get it!" Elrod snapped.

"Can we see him?" Elijah asked.

"Go in," Doctor Chen said, motioning with his hand toward the door.

Elijah entered the room and found John Stakes clay-faced and unbreathing, and he came out and repeated Doctor Chen's pronouncement to the unbelieving ears of his brother.

"He's dead," Elijah stated.

"We gotta go with 'em," Elrod answered.

"Well sure, all of us do, but in our own time, that's just life," Elijah agreed.

"No! Not with John, with the citizens! We've got to ride with 'em to Aspirations!" Elrod said. "I wasted John's time Elijah, his last precious minutes. I just saw them Indians on top of the ridge, and I panicked."

"It's not your fault," Elijah offered.

"Well, it didn't help any. We really tried though, didn't we?"

Elijah nodded emphatically. "Of course, we did! Elrod almost lost his back legs when he hit the fence, and you rode Elijah to the bone!"

Elrod entered John's room but did not stay long because his chest got tight and his eyes watered. He told himself this was due to the aroma of antiseptic, heavy and lingering in the room. "I'm sorry, John," Elrod muttered. "I wanted to get you here in one piece… We got your message out though." The tears increased their flow, and Elrod blinked them away as he made his promise. "We'll help the people of Aspirations; we'll see that they're taken care of. You did your part, just rest easy now, John."

Sixty-Nine

At this point in his tale Calafort stopped speaking, and after a short interval of silence he told his listeners, "Whatever happened between Crooked Taylor and Major McCleod after they rode out of town can only be guessed at now." He looked around the circle, then toward the approaching riders, who were now close enough for all of them to see, and not just the eyes of Moses Louis-May.

"I will end my story by saying," Father Calafort continued, "that I am thankful that the Lord in his wisdom and mercy, chose to send Lionel McCleod back to us, and not only for his survival, but also to demonstrate that at such a terrible hour, McCleod's light prevailed over Crooked's darkness."

Instead of absorbing this information in silence Ed immediately said, "Wait, Crooked ran for it? After all that he tried to just turn tail and run?"

"Crooked Taylor fled and McCleod followed," Father Calafort stated.

"How many times was McCleod shot?" Ed asked.

"Show some respect," Moses huffed.

"What respect? I rode under him; I wore the badge—"

"Yes, we all know about your badge—"

"I want to know how many times that crippled bastard shot him!" Ed demanded. "And I want to know how many rounds McCleod put in that son of a bitch in return."

"McCleod was shot once," Calafort said. "And if the Major

had not rode so far away from Aspirations, or had he had a horse, he would probably have survived."

This caused the group to pause and reflect, but as ever, Ed interrupted the solemnity by saying, "McCleod's a tough son of a bitch. To walk back all this way, I mean."

The group's members nodded in agreement, until there came a report from Moses.

"No movement up ahead. I can catch the twinkle when I walk back and forth. I think whatever it is it's staying put."

Calafort nodded, but repeated his sentiments from earlier as he said, "That's good. The riders are making progress behind us as well — they should not be too much longer."

The other members of the circle did not agree, as the riders' progress seemed insubstantial in the time they had been sitting and resting. But Calafort had spoken his piece, and so they continued to wait, trying to look relaxed, and not express their anxiety in any outward fashion.

Seventy

As the full strength of their posse rode forward, Moses Louis-May was the first to abandon caution, and Clarita gulped at his foolishness and her heart froze in her chest as her husband broke formation. But the day remained static and motionless, save for the snaking waves of heat rising from the sand.

Moses rode toward the place where Crooked had been killed, and there were not even vultures to disturb as he came upon the body.

The posse rode forward to join Moses, and all of them came to find Bradley lying supine, staring at the sky, his torso red and full of numerous bullet holes, while his infamous legs remained intact.

Ed walked around where he supposed the duel had happened, estimating where McCleod would have stood in order to shoot Crooked dead. "Right about here," Ed said, looking down his hand as though it held a pistol. "McCleod stood right about here and delivered all six, right in the chest." Ed spun and looked back in the direction of Aspirations then said, "And then McCleod hoofs it all the way back to civilization with a bullet in his lung. There won't ever be another Major McCleod."

"It seems he was sent by the Lord to protect us," Calafort said. Then, changing the subject he stated, "I am going to remain with the body. Any stragglers that arrive can look, but I will make sure he is not defiled, and I will see to it that the body is buried."

"Crooked don't deserve burying," Ed spat. "Let the coyotes

and the buzzards have him — if his meat won't make them sick."

"I am not burying him out of respect for the man he was," Calafort told Ed. "I am burying him out of respect for the men we are. We are not the sort of people to let bodies lay, no matter who's they were."

"Well, I ain't picking up a shovel for that rat," Ed said.

"You didn't pick up a gun neither," Moses chimed in.

"I came when I heard the message!" Ed snapped.

"I did not ask you to bury the body — nor anyone else," Father Calafort said. "I am perfectly able to do it myself." Father Calafort's tone left no room for compromise, and so the people in attendance of Crooked Taylor's body gawked for as long as they liked, and then slowly began to remount their tired animals and start the journey homeward.

The sun was red and swollen, sitting low in the sky when the last of the stragglers had had their look, and finally departed the body. The pink aura of sunset was interrupted by the flight of vultures, eager for Father Calafort to depart, but Father Calafort dug Crooked Taylor's grave deep and set what few stones he could find in the vicinity, atop the freshly churned dust.

Father Calafort wiped perspiration from his brow with the back of his sleeve, and then dusted his palms on the thighs of his jeans, before lacing his fingers together in prayer.

"Bradley Taylor fled, and Lionel McCleod followed," he began. "Forgive me, Father, for my lie, for I know that in truth, Lionel McCleod fled, and Bradley Taylor followed." Calafort lowered his eyes from heaven's waning light to the dusty grave he had dug. "None can know the reason for your suffering, and your spiteful relationship toward the world. However, I hope that your pain has come to an end, and that the lie I have told can heal the hearts of the men and women that need it. Forgive me, Father, for my lie, and forgive this man in whatever manner your divine wisdom knows to be best. May Bradley Taylor's soul be unburdened from its pain. Amen."

Night was nearly upon him by the time Father Calafort mounted and began the journey toward Aspirations, but the fires of his fellow travelers dotted the plains like fallen stars, and so he angled his horse towards the nearest one, and the hospitality it promised.

Seventy-One

The day the posse left to chase Crooked Taylor, Major Lionel McCleod passed away. But out of respect for the men and women hunting the outlaw, the funeral was not held until all of the members had returned.

Father Calafort had to deliver the sermon outdoors in order for the entire crowd to be accommodated, and it took another week before the hotels and saloons of Aspirations were no longer full of visitors.

The tale of Lionel McCleod and Crooked Taylor was repeated uncountable times, and each speaker filled in various details as they saw fit. But all knowledge of the final encounter between the two men, died alongside Crooked Taylor and Lionel McCleod.

Seventy-Two

After dispatching Arthur Coe and mounting his horse, Crooked Taylor caught sight of Lionel McCleod as McCleod exited a house and took cover against a low wall. Crooked held the horse's mane with his good hand, while he used the thumb and index finger on his ruined one to try to reload his lone remaining pistol. However, the hand was nearly useless, and shells rained down onto the ground as Crooked failed to feed rounds into the cylinder as he normally would.

Crooked abandoned the effort of reloading, instead yanking his frightened mare's mane about, until it angled its gallop toward Lionel McCleod.

McCleod had claimed a horse for himself, dispatching the rider and wrangling the frightened beast to a halt, and had his pistol been loaded, Crooked knew he would have had a decent shot.

Instead, Crooked sank down behind his horse's neck and swatted its rump with his injured hand despite the enormous pain it caused him, shouting in the animal's ear to run faster as Lionel McCleod turned his own animal around and began to flee.

Seventy-Three

Lunchtime saw a generous swell in customers, for the day was hot, but a breeze gently daubed the sweat on any citizens' brow. Bradley served tables, his feet like a dancer's as he waltzed between the mismatched furniture set around the room. But the customers were seated, and the courtyard remained empty and lifeless, and so he set down his apron and got his fiddle, positioning himself beneath his favorite tree, before he struck up a lively tune.

The music seemed to lubricate the crowd, for the noise increased immediately, and shouts of laughter began to exchange.

Bradley tried not to look down at his tips too often, but it was a good day, and the first shout of disaster could not even be heard against the backdrop of the merriment taking place in the courtyard.

Seventy-Four

The shouts became frantic, halting the music and the gaiety of the crowd, as a man crashed into a table and sent drinks and shards of glass shattering around him. The man stood up from the wreckage, having leapt from the balcony above, and he fired upward in the direction from which he had dropped, then shoved aside one of the women whose table he had landed upon, and began to run.

The young ranger with the serious face fired at the man as he sprinted across the courtyard and dove for cover behind the shady oak tree.

The young ranger fired frantically, working the lever of his Winchester up and down and sending hell at the man. Chips of bark snapped and blew from the tree, and the young ranger hit the man in the thigh and the buttocks, slowing him enough that his drunk comrades could pile onto him and hold him down until he was cuffed. The rangers were drunk and rowdy and beat the man badly before dragging him off toward the prison, but this was not the main concern of the people who witnessed the event.

One of the desperate rounds fired by the young ranger had caught the young boy in the spine and pitched him face-first onto the ground on top of his fiddle. The boy remained unconscious as the crowd around him assembled themselves, and while the bandit was cuffed and beaten, the wounded boy was carried from the courtyard, and up into a quiet room.

Seventy-Five

The young boy's father sat with him and held his hand, but Bradley writhed upon the bed, soaked in perspiration, and unable to make much sense, due to the whiskey the doctor had given him.

"His wound is tremendously painful. Use the whiskey liberally, whenever he needs it."

"Will he survive?"

"There's a fair chance."

"Can't you do anything else? Anything at all?"

The doctor shook his head and did not answer, and this was answer enough.

Seventy-Six

The hours rolled by like purgatory, baked dust beneath an unrelenting sun. The gait of his horse made Crooked terribly aware of his wounds, while his vision seemed splotchy, and vertigo plagued him from time to time. The sun counted out the minutes in agonizing slowness, slowly circumnavigating heaven's vault, while the distance between Crooked Taylor and Lionel McCleod grew smaller. And every time McCleod tried to alter his course, Crooked worked to angle him west, where there would be no chance for reinforcements.

Seventy-Seven

His horse was failing. McCleod felt the smoothness of its gait dropping away as his mount's breathing grew more ragged. Looking over his shoulder McCleod saw that Crooked was much too close behind him.

McCleod extracted a pistol and shot his horse in the rump, prompting a scream and a burst of speed, though this reinvigorated pace did not last for long, and within minutes of this tactic, the horse's legs were threatening to collapse beneath it once more.

Lionel McCleod employed a final tactic, and as his horse slowed to a lurch, he spun around and emptied the remaining five shots in his pistol's cylinder toward Crooked. Crooked hid behind his horse's neck and the creature was shot in the chest, neck and cheek, causing the horse to fall, and propelling Crooked Taylor from atop its back.

Dust swirled from the impact, and McCleod reached for his rifle in the scabbard on the saddle, but somehow Crooked was too fast for him.

"Hands up," Crooked wheezed. He lay on his side, training his pistol on Lionel McCleod with his lone usable hand, and as McCleod looked down at the man called Crooked Taylor, he could barely recognize what he saw.

Crooked Taylor's face was awash in blood and streaked with dirt and sweat. His shirt and pants were burgundy, soaked through with blood and caked over in dust. Crooked Taylor possessed the eyes of a madman and the smile of the devil, and the crippled bandit looked as though he was a corpse that had pulled itself out from a grave, refusing to surrender itself until some final deed was accomplished.

"You got me," McCleod said.

Crooked shook his head. "No." He tried to adjust his position where he lay, but when a spell of nausea overtook him, Crooked closed his eyes to let it pass, and McCleod reached for his rifle again. However, Crooked's gun was much too quick, and the nausea passed as he told McCleod, "Don't do that, that would be a bad way for it to end."

"How do you see it ending?" McCleod challenged. "You toy with me a bit, tell me everything you want to say then kill me?"

"Throw down your rifle." Crooked cocked the hammer and McCleod tossed his rifle away and shook his head. "You're scum, Taylor."

"Get down and load your pistol."

"…"

"Load it!"

McCleod was skeptical at first, and he moved slowly as he dismounted, but the offer was genuine, and he was free to unholster his pistol and slide rounds into its polished cylinder at his leisure.

Seventy-Eight

The room was dark, and the air was stale from not having been circulated in days. Lionel McCleod knocked quietly, but when there was no answer he removed his hat, smoothed down his hair with one hand, and entered the room where the wounded boy lay.

In the lightless interior there was only the bed and a single chair, occupied by the boy's father, who seemed to be dozing.

McCleod cleared his throat and the boy's father awoke, then patted the table beside him to locate his spectacles, before addressing the visitor. "This room is not to be disturbed, there is a sign on the door—"

"Yes, I know. But I am Private McCleod. I… I shot Michael Watson."

The man's face hardened, and he gripped the arms of the chair without rising. "While I cannot remove you from my hotel, I can at least ask you to get the hell out of my son's room."

"I want to explain."

"Then explain."

The exchange seemed to awaken the boy, but his eyes wandered the room without focus, and McCleod hoped that the boy's delirium was a result of the medication he had received, and not the fever he had supposedly developed.

"Watson's a dangerous criminal," McCleod explained. "He leapt from the balcony before I could arrest him, and I was afraid he would get away if I didn't act."

"How many rounds did you fire?" the boy's father snapped.

"Sir—"

"How many? And what did this man do? Was he so dangerous that you have the right to fire a dozen rounds into a crowd! Look at what you've done!" The boy's father stood up from the chair, his entire frame trembling as he struggled to control the tone of his voice.

"That man has already killed two people," McCleod stated. "If I let him go, then the next one he killed would have been my fault."

"What about my son? Isn't that your fault?"

Seventy-Nine

"That horse won't be any use to you; shot twice and so played out I'm surprised it's still standing; it's just jerky waiting to be jerked... Are you loaded yet?" McCleod looked up and Crooked lay on his belly, breathing shallowly and smiling with his pistol still trained on McCleod. "Every time I'm around you it makes me more and more angry that it took me this long to catch up. I don't know how you've done it."

McCleod ignored him and loaded his pistol, then held it hanging at his side. "If you lower your gun we can have a proper duel," McCleod said.

"First I want to show you something." Crooked used his mangled hand to open the pistol's cylinder, and he tilted it toward McCleod to show him that it was empty. "You should've taken the shot. You've been listening to an unarmed cripple all this time."

Crooked giggled, and McCleod's temper flared, but the moment of opportunity passed in the blink of an eye, as Crooked produced a lone bullet from his pocket, slid it into the gun, then replaced the cylinder into the side of the pistol.

"It took a lot to get here," Crooked said. He used his ruined hand to indicate the world around them, white and hot and purgatorial in its emptiness. "Did the ends justify the means?"

"I was young, Bradley—"

"I was younger."

"I was wrong."

"Yes. And you ran away and refused to face your destiny for so long, that in my pursuit of you, I became the sort of criminal that could no longer be ignored. A criminal that demanded the great Lionel McCleod's attention."

"I was wrong," McCleod repeated.

"I appreciate that you told my father that Michael Watson, the man you shot, was a murderer," Crooked said, his tone conversational. "It was devastating for me when I found out that you took my legs away by firing blindly at a horse thief; I'm glad my father died believing different."

"What do you want?"

Crooked grinned. "I want you to holster that pistol. I'll holster mine. Then we can either draw, or do it on a count, I'll leave that up to you."

"I don't need a count."

"Good. Me neither."

McCleod angrily stuffed his pistol into his holster, and this seemed to please Crooked, for he raised himself painfully up onto his knees, choking with the effort, as he tucked his pistol down into its holster, secure at his right hip.

Eighty

The world collapsed down to just eyes and fingers. Two men. Pistols holstered. The world around them motionless. McCleod stood with his shoulder to his target. Crooked knelt like a tripod on his bloody hand and knees.

"Why didn't you bring any crutches with you?" McCleod asked. "You could've stood like a man for our meeting."

Crooked twitched but did not pull. "Figures you'd put your shoulder to your target like a coward," Crooked replied. "That's all you've ever been."

"There's no glory to be had out here, Bradley — I don't know what you want."

"Yes, you do."

Crooked pulled his pistol and shot Lionel McCleod high in the side, tucking the bullet into the seam of his shirt's armpit. McCleod jerked from the impact before extracting his pistol and emptying all six rounds into Crooked Taylor's chest, pitching the outlaw backwards to lay face up at the sky.

McCleod touched the wound in his armpit and pulled away fingers red with blood. His first steps toward Crooked felt easy, but when he took a breath, his breath was snatched away by the pain. If not for the gurgle from the body, McCleod may have stood there until his coughing subsided, but instead, he lurched over to Crooked Taylor to stand victorious over top of him. "I've killed you, you son of a bitch," McCleod wheezed.

The body over which he stood was too ruinous to mention

individual injuries, but Crooked Taylor was not yet without life, and he shook his head at what McCleod told him.

"I did," McCleod asserted. "I killed you and I'm going to walk back to Aspirations and survive, just to spite you." McCleod began to cough, and he held his side in pain while stars burst across his vision, and Crooked Bradley Taylor expired, shaking his head in disagreement with Major Lionel McCleod.

Epilogue

A midnight wind set the forest to moaning as though the night itself were in pain. Behind a curtain of clouds, heaven was dark and featureless, with no stars to offer even a trace of illumination.

But Bradley knew the way, having already picked the tree. The tree was pretty, and Bradley wondered if this little bend in the road with its slope of wild grass might not be a place that in another lifetime, he could bring a girl that loved him. He could walk with her there, holding hands. Maybe he would dash away grinning mischievously after cracking an inappropriate joke. She would chase him, and they would end up rolling in the grass together, and they could look up at this tree, and the spot would be entirely transformed. But this was never to be his reality.

Sitting atop his horse, Bradley stopped beneath the selected tree, and threw the end of his rope over a low, sturdy-looking branch. He secured the rope, tightened the loop around his neck, and as he paused to reflect, he was interrupted by a voice; "Don't move or I'll shoot."

Bradley did as he was told, raising his hands and turning toward the voice, although he was still secured by his neck to the tree.

The voice was produced by a skinny Black man, outfitted in rags and without any shoes, his face heavily scarred, and his hair a disheveled mess. The man's clothes were so ragged that Bradley worried that during daylight hours, the clothes may not keep the man decent. The man's sole possession was a shotgun;

a shotgun so ancient that the shooter would be in equal danger to whomever he shot at.

"Get down off that horse. I don't want to hurt you, but I'm taking that horse."

Bradley laughed. "I don't think you know what you're doing."

"I've shot someone before. I don't want to, but if you don't get down off that horse right now, I'll do it again."

The Black man bristled at some unheard sound, and he turned his ear to the wind to listen. Bradley focused on listening, and at first, he wondered if the man had keener ears than he did, until Bradley could hear the distant bark of dogs.

"I can't get down," Bradley said.

"Then you're going to get killed," the man replied.

"I'm going to get killed if I do get down. I have a rope around my neck."

The Black man scrunched up his eyes and walked closer until he saw the noose.

"Oh. I won't shoot you then." He lowered the shotgun and stood, expectantly waiting.

"Don't look!" Bradley cursed.

"I ain't gonna turn my back on you. What if you pull a gun?"

"I'm not trying to fight for my life, I'm trying to end it!"

The howl of the hounds became more defined as the dogs approached, and the man's skin crawled. "Want me to shoot you? It'll make it faster and I need that horse."

"You said you didn't want to shoot me!"

"I don't, but I need that horse. I'll let you hang if you'll be quick, but I can't wait too long."

Bradley looked down at the horse. One slap and the man could have it and Bradley would never have another concern again. "I don't want to rush this. I'm not so sure any more," Bradley admitted.

"Well did you come out here to think or did you come out here to hang? I need that damned horse!" The sound of the approaching hounds seemed to encourage the shotgun to focus on Bradley again, but the man's eyes were wide and pleading. "Come with me and I'll help you hang properly, or you can get down, they won't hurt you. Please, I need that horse."

"I'm gonna untie this," Bradley said, arriving at a decision. "Come and hop on."

The man approached the horse and tried to hop up behind Bradley, but the horse got frightened and stepped forward such that Bradley slid off her back and began to hang. His eyes bulged and he clawed at the noose around his windpipe, when the Black man came to his rescue. The man grabbed Bradley's atrophied legs and held him up, slackening the line so Bradley could untie the rope. And without setting him down, the Black man carried Bradley over to his mount, depositing him back in the saddle.

"Do I ride in front or behind?" the man asked, once Bradley was situated.

"Ride behind. You're plenty strong to hold on," Bradley said.

The man jumped up successfully this time, and he wrapped his arms around Bradley's torso, as Bradley slapped the horse's rump to start it moving.

"What's your name?" Bradley asked the man hugging him from behind.

"I'm Hugo," the man said in his ear. "And you?"

"Bradley Taylor. But people call me *Crooked*."

The End.

Preview to: *Bug* — The Calhoun Account

Eleven years after the siege of Aspirations, Texas and Bug Calhoun finds himself settled on a small ranch in western Arkansas with his wife and two children. Bug reminisces for hours about the siege because he figures his life's greatest excitement is behind him. But read on, because a series of gunshots at midnight and the eruption of a house fire... Well, that's no way for a family man's life to remain dull and uninteresting.

Experience a special sneak preview of the next novel in the *Crooked* Taylor universe: ***Bug — The Calhoun Account.***

Chapter One

"Papa! Papa, I hear gunshots!"

"Come in here, sweetie," Bug called out. Bug reached over in bed and grabbed onto Patricia's hand, squeezing it firmly, and he received a firm squeeze in return.

The bedroom door swung open and collided with the doorframe like a clap of thunder, and little Celeste scurried barefoot across the wooden floorboards before diving onto the foot of her parents' bed.

"Mama, Papa—"

"You two stay here," Bug said. He kicked the heavy duvet covers from around his legs and rolled out of bed, clad only in his ratty long john underwear.

"Celeste, where's your brother?" Patricia asked her daughter as Celeste crawled up the bed and into her mother's embrace.

"I don't know — still in his room?"

"I'm getting him," Bug said.

The curtains were drawn so the darkness in the room was all but complete, but even so Bug navigated the cluttered floor with ease. Feeling a shirt underneath his bare toes, Bug stooped down, picked up the shirt, and stuffed his arms into the sleeves. He felt on his shoulders that the seams were inside out, but Bug disregarded this triviality in his haste.

Outside the bedroom, large caliber rifles thumped intermittently, while the crack of pistols filled the intervening gaps, destroying the night's silence.

"Ardner! Ardner, where are you?" Patricia called.

"Mama! Mama!" Ardner's voice replied from the room next door.

"Stay there, pal, I'm coming!" Bug hollered. Stumbling around in the darkness, Bug cursed under his breath and soon abandoned whatever it was he was searching for. Clad only in long johns and his inside out shirt, Bug raced from the room, and returned a moment later carrying his young son Ardner in his arms.

"Stay here with your mother, both of you."

"Bug, you can't go out there, there's gunshots!" Patricia said.

"Listen, I may go outside without proper pants," Bug said, sweeping his vision across their dark bedroom and failing again to find his pants, "but I ain't going outside without a gun, I'm not crazy." Bug fetched a lever action rifle hanging from a hook nailed beside the door, then stepped out into the dark hallway, before pausing to turn back and address Patricia once more. "Patricia, just in case... I love you, honey."

"Dammit, Bug, don't say that! What sort of terrible luck are you trying to bring down on us?"

Bug closed the bedroom door against the anger of his wife, but it did little to diminish the sounds of her tirade.

Bug strode across the dark floor of the humble cabin and arrived at the outside door where he took a moment to stuff his feet into his boots. While he did so, Bug turned the lever action rifle towards the wan light of the moon as it filtered through the kitchen window and examined the weapon in his hands.

"I should've lit a candle," Bug muttered. Regardless, his fingers were adept enough to crack open the breach of the rifle and feel the round situated within the rifle's mechanism, ready to be fired.

Voices called back and forth from outside the small cabin, and the gunshots accompanying the voices suggested a multitude of attackers. As Bug's breathing began to accelerate, his eyes searched the gloominess of the main room of the cabin. Locating Patricia's sun hat above the door, Bug fetched it down and covered his mouth over with the hat, breathing in and out of the bowl of the hat in great whooping gasps, as he fought against his instinct to hyperventilate.

"Find your breath, Bug… Just find your breath, your family needs you."

The bowl of the hat served poorly for hyperventilation, but the focus on his breathing seemed to mitigate Bug's growing hysteria, until a flash of light startled him, and nearly caused his skeleton to leap free of his skin.

An orange bloom of fire exploded across the kitchen floor, dousing the legs of the wooden chairs and table in its flammable contents, as the devilish flames licked and sputtered upon the throw rug where it landed.

Bug jammed Patricia's hat onto the crown of his head, then raced over to the torch. He picked up the flaming stick that had been wrapped in cheap fabric and set alight, but as he approached the broken kitchen window to throw the torch outside, another torch burst through the same window and landed on the floor as well.

"Patricia! Patricia, get the kids out of there; we need to leave right now!"